D1373622

The Single Gal's Guide to
SHOPPING FOR A
GREAT GUY

Singles, it's time to re-evaluate our
shopping habits and shopping lists!

LJB

The Single Gal's Guide to
SHOPPING FOR A GREAT GUY

Valuing your worth as a single girl who's living and looking for love in a cheap, sex-selling world

Tiffany Yvonne Grant

THE SINGLE GAL'S GUIDE TO SHOPPING FOR A GREAT GUY
VALUING YOUR WORTH AS A SINGLE GIRL WHO'S LIVING AND
LOOKING FOR LOVE IN A CHEAP, SEX-SELLING WORLD

iUniverse books may be ordered through booksellers or by contacting:

iUniverse
1663 Liberty Drive
Bloomington, IN 47403
www.iuniverse.com
1-800-Authors (1-800-288-4677)

Because of the dynamic nature of the Internet, any web addresses or links contained in this book may have changed since publication and may no longer be valid. The views expressed in this work are solely those of the author and do not necessarily reflect the views of the publisher, and the publisher hereby disclaims any responsibility for them.

Any people depicted in stock imagery provided by Thinkstock are models, and such images are being used for illustrative purposes only. Certain stock imagery © Thinkstock.

ISBN: 978-1-4917-6651-4 (sc)
ISBN: 978-1-4917-6652-1 (e)

Library of Congress Control Number: 2015908106

Print information available on the last page.

iUniverse rev. date: 8/5/2015

This book is dedicated to …

Christopher Burnett Grant
February 16, 1983 - September 26, 2013

Chris was my amazing little brother. We were like two peas in a pod. He was one of my best friends, and we were each other's biggest fans. In 2013, the Lord called Chris home after he suffered a heart attack while driving to work. He was only thirty. Referred to as a gentle giant, Chris was a selfless, funny, talented, intelligent sweetheart. He was the reason I refused to hear girls say that "all men are dogs," because he was a great guy! We shared so much—beliefs, hopes, and dreams. We planned to champion so many causes together and to build our business empire (CNT). But the Lord had a different plan for us both. I am so thankful for the thirty years of unconditional love, gut-busting laughs, loyal friendship, loving encouragement, and lasting memories that God gave us, and I will cherish them forever. I was blessed to have you in my life, Chris, and felt so lucky to be your big sis. My heart beams with pride at the very thought of you! I love you, lil bro, and

I miss you with all my heart. Thank you for believing in your big sis. I pray that I continue to make you proud!

RoShawnda Rachelle Little

September 21, 1977 - March 21, 2011

Shawnda was also one of my best friends and was my sis from another miss (Avaleen, LOL). She lost a brave battle with cancer in 2011. From twelve to thirty-three, from middle school to college, from victories to tragedies, we experienced it all. Shawnda had this light that shined so bright on so many, and a smile that could illuminate a room. Even at her darkest hour, her positivity and faith never wavered. Shawnda, you showed me the true meaning of authentic friendship and sisterhood and how to persevere through life's tests. Our friendship is proof that women can love, encourage, have an occasional spat, and push each other without gossip, competition, and drama. I miss you, sista, but I can smile knowing that you and Chris are up in Heaven together having a blast! Hug Jesus for me!

PS—I also have some of the most amazing shopping gals/ girlfriends on the planet. I love you all to the moon and back! Without your encouragement, love, support, and honesty, The Single Gal's Guide *would not be possible. I also dedicate this book to each of you.*

Contents

Introduction

Question: Tiff, so what is *The Single Gal's Guide to Shopping for a Great Guy* about anyway?

Answer: Well, gals, I am so glad you asked. But first, let's start with what it's *not* about.

The Single Gal's Guide is not about hating singleness. It's not about living life like it's over because you're by yourself. This is not a male-bashing book, because all men are not dogs, from another planet, or out to harm you, hurt you, cheat on you, control you, use, abuse, or misuse you. *The Single Gal's Guide* is not a self-help book, although you might just help yourself by reading it. This is not a how-to book either, but prayerfully it will show you how to be a better you.

The Single Gal's Guide was written specifically for single gals by me—a single gal. So, ladies, if any of the following describes who you are, how you feel, and things that you do, this book is definitely for you!

- single and loving it or single and anxiously waiting and watching the biological clock ticktock

- single with low self-esteem or single and extremely into yourself
- single and saving sex for marriage or single and recommitting to a life of celibacy
- single and giving it away or single and struggling from night to night to keep 'em closed
- single due to divorce or single because death made you part
- single grandmothers, mothers, godmothers, daughters, sisters, aunts, nieces, cousins, friends, BFFs, besties, bosses, coworkers, frenemies, and enemies
- single and never had a ring on it, about to get a ring on it, or praying and fasting for somebody to put a ring on it
- single and beautifully black, white, brown, or any other gorgeous color on the spectrum

(*Disclaimer*: If you are married but separated, you are *not* single. If you are dating and not engaged, you are *still* single.)

The Single Gal's Guide is a shopping analogy to living single and looking for love—God's way. Its goal is to help singles navigate through a sex-saturated society that says you have to sell yourself cheap, compromise your market value, and display your goods to catch a great deal (i.e., a great guy). *The Single Gal's Guide* is about the importance of loving God and reflecting on His Word while loving yourself and respecting yourself in your singleness.

The Single Gal's Guide will examine how to date, find a mate, be a good friend, and love good men. It will confirm, convict, challenge, convince, and maybe even change how you see yourself and others; and change how you walk through this single season of your life. You will laugh. You might cry. You may even say "Ouch" or shout "Amen!"

The underlying theme of *The Single Gal's Guide* is to wait until the wedding or to live a celibate life until you find Mr. Right and a covenant makes you his wife. But until you say "I do," *The Single Gal's Guide* will help you shop, search, and select the one who was specifically designed just for you. Prayerfully you will read it over and over again and then share it with a girlfriend.

Attention, shoppers, ladies, gals, divas, lovelies, girls, beloveds, beauties, girlies, sistas, and friends (and any other loving term we call women we adore): *The Single Gal's Guide* is about to begin. Prepare for all that's in *store*!

Enjoy the shopping trip!

Tiff

Throughout *The Single Gal's Guide*, be on the lookout for the following:

Chapter Checkouts
After the sale is closed, customers get to take items with them, right? Each chapter in *The Single Gal's Guide* has a checkout section that will give you the opportunity to jot down what you've taken away from the chapter. Use this section to highlight what you liked, learned, and plan to live out (that is, apply to your life).

Disclaimers
When a product lists disclaimers, the goal is to spell out clearly the intent in hopes of preventing its misuse or a misunderstanding of its purpose. Throughout *The Single Gal's Guide*, you will read disclaimers that will ensure you're clear on the chapter's intent.

Fine Print

Sometimes shoppers make purchases without reading the fine print first. Although it's small, the fine print is often the most critical information on the page. It provides important clarification or details that could keep the shopper from making a poor choice or harmful purchase. Be sure to read the fine print throughout *The Single Gal's Guide*.

Chapter Warranties

Each chapter in *The Single Gal's Guide* is covered by a warranty. Warranties are promises, commitments, agreements, or covenants that manufacturers provide on their products. Warranties typically cover purchases for a specified period of time and are either limited or extended. Luckily, chapters throughout *The Single Gal's Guide* are covered by warranties that our manufacturer (our Heavenly Father) has guaranteed. *His* warranties (His precious and powerful Word) are unlimited and cover us all for a lifetime!

Chapter 1

The Start of the Shopping Trip

Ladies, we can't start *The Single Gal's Guide* without laying a foundation about why women are hardwired to shop, and when and where the notion of shopping all began. I know. I know. Not all women live to or even like to shop, but we *all* have had extensive experience shopping in some form, whether by choice or for necessity. Even if collecting clothes and stashing shoes is not your thing, some of us prefer to peruse for purses, pick produce, hunt for home goods, or grab groceries and go.

So let's go back to the beginning—the ABCDs!

A Is for Apple—The First Woman's First Shopping Trip

If I were to use my illustrative imagination, I believe that the history of women and shopping goes back as far as 4000 BC. Shortly after God created Eve, she visited the world's first farmer's market, the glorious Garden of Eden.

While picking fresh fruits and various veggies for her hardworking husband, Adam, Eve was approached by the very first slimy, smooth-talking salesman: Satan the Serpent. In fewer than six Bible verses, that ole sneaky snake convinced Eve to give into gimmicks, and she fell for the sell. That apple was the first thing a woman bought that she did not need! God had granted Eve *free* access to any of the other fruit from all the other trees in the Garden. But no! Eve picked the most expensive fruit at the farmer's market, the one from the forbidden tree. (That's like having a coupon for free shoes but choosing to buy a $2,000 pair instead. Yep, certifiably and undeniably cray-cray-crazy!)

Eve's poor pick illustrates how women have been falling for false advertising and making hasty, ill-advised purchases for centuries, grabbing things we know we don't need and can't afford. To this day, we still dismiss that little voice telling us to walk away from that hard-to-resist item. Instead, we buy it and then spend months, even years, paying for it. Eve may not have paid cash or credit for that apple, but it definitely came at a cost. Come to think about it, ladies, we have been paying for Eve's apple ever since she picked it by way of sin, painful childbirth, cramps, etc. Talk about buyer's remorse, a whole lot of interest, and a heck of a repayment term!

Disclaimer: Having worked in retail and sales, I am in no way implying that all salespeople are slick-talking snake-oil salesmen. But we all know there are some slithering through stores!

B Is for Birthday List—A Girl's First Shopping List

Fast-forward from the beginning of labor pains (thanks a lot, Eve!) to the first birthday you remember, which is probably around age five. Back then, Mom or Dad may have asked you what you wanted on your special day. Because you were learning to read and write at the time, you might have tried to jot your little wishes and wants down on a birthday list.

Ladies, this was unofficially your first shopping list. The only differences were you weren't buying a thing on it, and there was a strong possibility you weren't getting everything on it either. And much like your shopping list these days, your first list was probably full of stuff you saw on TV, or stuff you saw other people with, or stuff that was way outside the family budget, or stuff you just wanted and didn't really need. The birthday list helped to birth the habit of listing your needs, likes, wants, wishes, desires, and dreams. And whether we jot them down or not, we all still keep our wish-and-want lists in the backs of our minds.

That being said, think back to when you were five, and jot down the first three things you think you would have wanted on that birthday. We will revisit this list soon!

1.
2.
3.

C Is for Carts—A Girl's First Shopping Trip

The first shopping trip for many of us took place in Mama's shopping cart. You see—secretly Mama dreaded taking us shopping with her because she knew we would want any and everything in sight. So Mama, in her infinite wisdom, devised a plan where she would:

1. sneak to the store and leave us at home;
2. threaten us—from the house to the car to the front door of the store—not to beg for stuff "because she did not have money for it"; or
3. put us in the shopping cart to ensure our safety, limit her spending, and maintain her sanity.

Despite Mama's threats and confinement, we still reached for, grabbed for, and whined for stuff we saw and wanted. Shopping with Mama planted a seed that would grow gradually as we grew up. That seed would cultivate our own shopping habits.

D Is for Dolls—Our First Buy

Let's go back to *B* for a minute. One of the first things you might have put on your birthday list when you were five was a doll. (At five years old, a doll was definitely on my wish-and-want list.) As soon as most little girls had access to a few dollars or knew that Mama did, they wanted to spend it on a baby or a Barbie doll.

Why a doll? Well, little boys were raised to be tough— crashing toy cars, fighting action figures, and building blocks into towers only to demolish them. Little girls were the exact opposite. We were taught to be sweet – loving and nurturing to our dolls, living imaginary lives as wives and mommies, and playing dress up as princesses and brides. We lived vicariously through our dolls, and in some ways we still do.

So there you have it—the ABCDs of how the shopping trip began, from the first woman to our first experiences as little girls. So I guess shopping is both biblical and genetic, gals. (Ha! I am sure some study shows it somewhere.)

But now that we are all grown up, the ABCDs have slightly different meanings.

The *Apple* relates to how we shop for and pick out the wrong fruit (men and relationships) versus following God's clear instruction (His Word). Like Eve, oftentimes we let Satan and his cunning temptation influence the selection/shopping process, rather than letting God be our personal shopper and making the perfect selection for us based on His purpose for our lives.

The *Birthday List* represents the early start of a habit of many single shoppers: list making, either mental or written. These lists are stacked full of needs, wants, and desires for our ideal man and the ideal relationship. But like our childhood birthday list, too few things on this list are necessary, while some of the items are unrealistic and ultimately unattainable.

Mama's shopping *Cart* reflects a single gal's desire for love, and how she will beg and whine to God for a whole lot of stuff that she does not need in a man. Like the young girl in the cart, we are coasting through life's aisles, reaching for options that may not be good for us. Like Mama, God has told us what we can and cannot have, but we continue to ask and pray and try to grab for what we shouldn't have anyway. We roll by what's good for us while settling for what's on display or is conveniently located on a low shelf, where it quickly catches the eye.

Dolls provided role models for a lifestyle we aspired to—love, marriage, and the baby carriage. Barbie lived the ideal life! Sister, friend, mommy, wife. Shiny long hair always in place. Flawless makeup never smudged on her face. Highly coveted breasts and the perfect size. Clothes, shoes, and plenty to accessorize. Barbie had her own dollhouse, condo, swimming pool, Jeep, and Porsche—plus dogs, cats, and even a horse.

We loved Barbie and all our baby dolls because we loved the roles they represented, that of wife and mommy. So as we matured, we went from playing with a plastic Ken to longing for a real, life-size version of him. But only a plastic couple could live a perfect life with a perfect match. As we grew, we learned that life isn't perfect and neither are we. And neither should we expect our mate to be.

Now that you know your ABCDs, you can start this shopping trip with me!

Chapter 1 Warranty

Read Genesis 3:18-24.

Ladies, the longing for love and little ones was a seed planted in many of us before we were conceived. From the beginning, God created woman to desire the love of a man. This was the reason why He made Eve—to support and love Adam and bear his fruit. Moreover, women have been going on shopping trips for centuries! This is evident with Eve's shopping spree on the wrong tree. But the beauty in Eve's mistake is that despite her picking the wrong fruit, God still made her fruitful by placing Jesus, you, and me in her lineage.

Chapter 1 Checkout

What I liked and learned while reading this chapter:

1.
2.
3.

What I want to live out and apply to my life going forward:

1.
2.
3.

Chapter 2

The Shopping List

Girlies, regardless of whether we've written it down or not, most of us shoppers keep a shopping list. We usually have an idea of what we're going to get before we go hunting for it, right? The typical grocery shopping list contains the following:

- stuff we have to get (e.g., nonnegotiables like toilet paper)

- stuff we want if we happen to find it (e.g., a new conditioner we heard about)
- stuff we really don't need that isn't good for us (e.g., junk food)
- stuff that is good for us that we really don't want (e.g., brussels sprouts)

Single ladies tend to do the same thing when "shopping" for a single man—with our wish-and-want list in mind. *Every* gal has had that infamous list, the what-she-wants-in-a-man list. You know—the ideal mate's characteristics, dos and don'ts, pros and cons, nonnegotiables and must-haves and can't-haves, the turn-ons and turnoffs, the A-to-Zs, the 1-2-3s, the top ten, the top twenty, and so forth.

Like our typical grocery shopping list, these lists are full of the *got-to-get* items, the *I'll-take-them-if-he-has-them* items, the *not-good-for-me-but-I-sure-want-them* items, *and* the *looks-good-on-the-list-but-I-know-I-really-don't-want-them* items.

Just for fun, take a few minutes to jot down the top ten things you want in a man. Be thorough! Be honest!

1.
2.
3.
4.
5.
6.
7.

8.
9.
10.

Honestly, I've had a list or two or ten throughout my life. Want a good laugh? Let's travel through time and look at mine. (Don't judge me!)

Tiff's Prelist (Prior to 1991)
By age twelve, I had already been married and divorced several times—according to my vivid imagination. This prelist has all my former last names. I'm keeping my "ex-husbands" anonymous, to protect their identities.

➤ Tiffany James (1981)
➤ Tiffany Jackson (1982)
➤ Tiffany Brown and Tresvant (1983)
➤ Tiffany Huxtable (1984)
➤ Tiffany DeBarge (1985)
➤ Tiffany Cool J (1986)
➤ Tiffany Jackson (1987—I believed in second chances. There was just something about the way he made me feel.)
➤ Tiffany B. Sure (1988)
➤ Tiffany Ice/Van Winkle (1989)
➤ Tiffany Devoe (1990)

Technically before age thirteen, I did not have lists. I was still into playing with Barbies. Boys were gross and annoying. But in the era of MTV and Video Soul, I started to identify my likes and dislikes.

Tiff's List @ 13 (Eighth Grade/1992)—The Double Cs
(not to be confused with my nonexistent cup size in
the '90s)

- ✓ cute
- ✓ cute clothes

Yes, low expectations and low standards. But hey, in my
house at thirteen, all I could have was a wish list. I was
so young I couldn't really get to know—and didn't want
to get to know—the inner boy, so all I had was the outer.
Besides, at that age, boys who liked you teased and taunted
you. In response, we girls would scold and slap them in
public, while we crushed on them and called them cute
in private.

Tiff's List @ 18 (Twelfth Grade/1996)—The Straight As

- ✓ attractive
- ✓ athletic
- ✓ access to cash
- ✓ attends church
- ✓ access to an automobile

Aside from boys, I was actually into academics, but notice
that making As was not on my list. Talk about superficial!
At eighteen, for me the outside still counted more than the
inside. Fine and popular trumped kind and intelligent.
The geek was overlooked. The jock was overrated. I was
no different! My list was longer but lacked substance. Still,
what do you expect from a high-school senior without a

care in the world who was not looking to get married? Who was just looking to have fun while preparing for college and a bright future full of fine jocks and frat boys. (Texas A&M, College Station, here I come! Whoop! Gig 'em, Aggies, class of 2000!)

Tiff's List @ 24 (Postcollege/2002)—The Gots and the Nots

- ✓ got to be tall
- ✓ got to be in shape
- ✓ got to be well groomed
- ✓ got to have a car
- ✓ got to have goals
- ✓ got to have a job
- ✓ got to be intelligent
- ✓ got to go to church
- ✓ not have kids
- ✓ not live with Mama

By the time I was twenty-four, college was a memory. I was young and driven, so I desired my equal—a young man who was ready to hook life by the horns. A young professional who was a playmaker looking to score a touchdown with the American dream. I was young and superficial, believing that the career made the man. Confidence and arrogance were attractive. Sweet and hardworking did not have a chance! And so I missed out on what could have been meaningful relationships, potential mates, and loving marriages many, many times because of my big ole mouth and my big ole list.

Tiff's List @ 30 (After Graduate School/2008)—The "Past Ready" List

- ✓ relationship with God
- ✓ values family
- ✓ good sense of humor
- ✓ well groomed
- ✓ intelligent
- ✓ honest and trustworthy
- ✓ eye-to-eye height
- ✓ no more than one child
- ✓ able to support himself financially

When I turned thirty, my list was a tad shorter but had more substance. I had the itchy ring finger, the ticking biological clock, and parents who kept reminding me that they wanted grandkids within the century. No kids. No husband. No husband. No kids. I felt past ready, but I eventually realized that God was still preparing me, and that I was not as ready as I thought I was.

Tiff's List @ 30+ (Today)—*T-He* List

- ✓ I want exactly who God wants for me!

Yep, that was it! I *finally* realized that I needed to *throw out my list*! Now at thirty-something, my list is shorter than it was when I was thirteen. But I believe it has everything that I need on it.

Why?

15

God knows me. (Heck, He created me.) He knows my heart. He knows my future. He knows my wants. He knows my needs. He knows my hopes. He knows my dreams. He knows the right timing. He knows the right age. He knows what I like. He knows my taste. So I trust Him. And I'm willing to wait patiently because I believe that one day He'll send Mr. Right right to me.

His list is t-He list.

Single ladies, we all keep a list in the backs of our minds of what and who we want. We set our standards and then sift through our options, checking off our lists of criteria that we deem important. Don't get me wrong. We all should have standards and we all should stand by them. But if we were honest, our top ten might have one item that covers the Christian category and nine others that are superficial.

What if God had a great guy for you but chose to give him to someone else because that man did not measure up to your list? Ironically, the most perfect man in the world for many of us could not live up to the standards we've set. Let's look at Jesus:

- ✓ lived from house to house
- ✓ walked everywhere—no wheels and an occasional donkey
- ✓ was most likely not the most well-groomed man
- ✓ was always surrounded by "His boys"
- ✓ left his steady carpentry job and depended on others for His necessities

✓ was not considered educated
✓ was born in a barn and raised in the hood
✓ chose to hang out with people who many would consider beneath them
✓ walked around healing people and raising them from the dead (you know you would have thought He was certifiably cray-cray-crazy)
✓ had a mother who told people she was a virgin when she gave birth to her son (Future mother-in-law? Most of us would have run!)

My point is that we need to throw out our lists. Picking a man is different from picking bruise-free fruits and veggies or a killer pair of heels. So stop concentrating on your list and expecting a man to measure up to what *you* put on it. Just like any shopping list, you don't need everything you put on the list or in your shopping cart. Let God build your list to ensure that the man measures up to what God desires for you. Work on being who God expects you to be: a loving, godly woman of integrity who pursues her personal goals and works to realize her dreams. If you can master that and leave the matchmaking up to God, He will exceed your expectations and send you the man of your dreams.

Chapter 2 Warranty

Read Proverbs 31.

So, before you go drafting a list of what you expect, try meeting the following expectations. How do you line up with this list?

- ✓ noble character
- ✓ loyal and trustworthy
- ✓ caring and loving
- ✓ hardworking and helpful
- ✓ wise and knows her worth
- ✓ supportive, submissive, and selfless
- ✓ sympathetic to the needs of others
- ✓ strong, skillful, and smart
- ✓ attracts a respectful man (mainly because she respects herself) and demands respect from others
- ✓ knows when to speak and when not to speak (not loud, nagging, rude, gossipy or with an attitude)
- ✓ takes care of home (the house *and* the hubby, if you know what I mean)
- ✓ has the love and respect of her family and friends

If you strive to be everything on the Proverbs 31 list, God will bring a man into your life who will recognize that you are all that and a bag of chips (the healthy kind, not the junky ones), and everything else on *his* shopping list!

Chapter 2 Checkout

What I liked and learned while reading this chapter:

    1.

    2.

    3.

What I want to live out and apply to my life going forward:

    1.

    2.

    3.

Chapter 3

Protecting the Purse

Friends, four things truly enhance the shopping experience:

1. *Good girlfriend*—the honest one who will say when you look fab or drab. The one who will tell you to look but don't touch because it costs way too much. The one who will help you hunt down your size and will celebrate your new items like you just won a prize.

2. *Plenty of time*—time to window-shop, try on options, pose and walk the dressing-room catwalk, compare sales by store hopping, eat in the food court and chat, place possible purchases on hold, and return impulse buys before leaving the mall (maybe because you found it cheaper somewhere else because you had ample time to do so).

3. *Comfy, cute shoes*—so that sore toes won't become a distraction or deterrent from finding a deal or

discount, and will allow you to walk through all the stores in style while accumulating mall miles.

4. *Purse*—to carry all the important shopping essentials, including but not limited to coupons, sales ad with the item you want circled, cash or a checkbook as well as credit or debit cards, and everything else that a gal carries in her handbag.

While options one through three are not always possible, option four is not optional. Plenty of us have shopped in stressful shopping conditions: alone, in a hurry, in hurting heels. But few to none have shopped without a handbag (purse or pouch, wallet or wristlet, etc.).

What's so special about a purse?

A woman's purse is one of her most precious, prized possessions. It holds her whole life within its clasps, buttons, or zipper. Makeup. Cell phone. IDs. Keys. Driver's license. SS card. Wallet with cash, checks, credit, debit, and ATM cards. Everything she needs is in her purse. Everything she values is in her purse. Regardless of its design, material, size, or color, a woman's purse is invaluable to her. Whether it's an expensive Dooney & Burke or a pricey Coach, a $19.99 Target handbag or a "hot" buy from the hair salon, a purse sticks closer to a woman than some of her girlfriends.

So what if you were out shopping and you accidentally laid your purse down and forgot where you left it?

You would think you'd lost your mind! You would go straight into panic mode, frantically retracing your steps, praying as you race from place to place that you'll find your purse. Losing your purse would cause stress, sweat, tears, headache, heartache, and the recurring fear of your precious, prized possession being rummaged through, its contents taken and discarded and lost forever. You would go to pieces because it's your purse!

So if your purse were lost and then found, what would you do?

You would be thankful that your precious, prized possession was found safe, untouched, intact, and containing all its valuables. You would put it in a safe spot where you could spot it easily, and you would guard it carefully. After knowing how it felt to lose your purse, you would keep it closed and closer than before. Not just anyone would be able to touch it or poke through it. You would not let any casual acquaintance open it or grab what was inside. You would not leave it lying around with your ID, wallet, and other treasures exposed and unprotected. You would not set it down and walk away from it. You would trust very few people with your purse because you know that you're the only one who truly values its contents. You would protect it because it's your purse!

So lovelies, why don't we value our precious bodies like we value our purses?

Why do some of us let just anyone rummage through us, take from us, and discard us?

Some of us leave our bodies (our precious, prized possessions) out for the world to see, and then we have the nerve to get mad when folks label us cheap or a knockoff. We allow our bodies to be passed around like secondhand shoes or hand-me-down handbags. We don't guard and protect ourselves like we guard and protect our purses.

We lie around with anybody, allowing them to pick our pockets, rummage through our purses, and take the most valuable things from us. Things like our hearts, our self-esteem, and our self-worth. At times, we lose our IDs (identities), our credit (character and reputation), and even our money. Some of us lose our minds and our freedom (bricks through windshields, theft, excessive calling and texting, breaking and entering, threats and stalking all can lead to jail time).

Ladies, it's time for us to stop valuing material stuff (purses and pouches) while devaluing our physical stuff (private parts). Beauties, value your bodies. To God, you are a precious, prized possession. Treat your body like you treat your purse. Hold it close, guard it, and only lay it down or open it up for its rightful owner—your husband. Your handbag only has one rightful owner, doesn't it? You don't just use it and then hand it around to others to use, do you? You don't let people who you barely know or trust take stuff from it or even handle your handbag, do you? So stop passing your "purse" around or allowing others to pick through it. Love yourself and protect yourself like you would your purse!

Chapter 3 Warranty

Read 1 Corinthians 6:19–20.

According to 1 Corinthians 6:19–20, our bodies are God's temple and were bought with a price—Jesus's precious blood! This means that we are expensive and invaluable too. Because of the price He paid for us, God wants us to glorify Him with our bodies, not give our bodies to a whole bunch of *hims*! When you buy a pricey purse, you take care of it so that it remains in great condition and fulfills its purpose. You don't buy an expensive handbag to share. God sees me and you in the exact same way. He bought us for His purpose! So show God's temple a little R-E-S-P-E-C-T!

From now on, consider your purse/private parts/precious, prized possession the equivalent of the most expensive purse on the planet. So expensive that it's adorned in solid gold and equipped with a diamond-studded lock that has only one special key. It's so expensive that someone looking for a cheap bargain couldn't and wouldn't want to touch it, for fear he would damage it and be forced to pay a hefty price for it. Consider your purse so valuable that most will only admire it and dream of owning it. Imagine that it is so expensive it could not be knocked off and sold for a fraction of its value. So expensive that very few could have access to it. So expensive that its owner (your husband) will guard that purse and protect it, like he protects his own wallet.

Fine Print: Please know that if you have already passed your purse around, it's okay. Don't be ashamed and don't feel that you are unworthy or devalued. But please don't continue to let anyone rummage through you. God forgives you and He will restore you. He loves you and He sees your value. You are worth the wait, ladies! Despite your past, you are His precious, prized possession. Reclaim ownership of your purse, guard it, and keep it close. And until you get married, commit to celibacy and keep it closed. Remember—not everyone values you as the precious, prized possession that you are. Protect your purse!

Chapter 3 Checkout

What I liked and learned while reading this chapter:

    1.
    2.
    3.

What I want to live out and apply to my life going forward:

    1.
    2.
    3.

Chapter 4

Clipping Coupons

Gals, when you were growing up, did your mom clip coupons? Mine sure did! I remember watching her sift through the Sunday paper, scissors in hand. By the time she was done, that paper looked like a kindergarten art project. Once she had completely dissected the paper, she would store her coupons in a plastic baggie in her purse and carry them around until she needed them. At the store, Mom would proudly present the coupons to the cashier and brag to us about all the money she had saved. To this day, Mom still clips coupons and is still the best penny pincher I know. Growing up with this thrifty example definitely sowed a seed in my life because I rarely shop without a coupon in hand or in my handbag.

A smart and savvy shopper knows the importance of a good deal. That's why, like my mom, she hunts for and hangs on to those really good coupons. Whether it was from the Sunday paper, a monthly mailer, an online ad, or a text message deal that you can't pass up, we have all redeemed a coupon.

The value of coupons vary.

There are certain coupons that are considered as good as gold, while others really aren't worth the time it takes to cut the sucker out of the newspaper, get into the car, drive to the store, and stand in line to redeem it.

For example, a highly coveted coupon might read:

Everything is 75% OFF

Including sale and clearance items

NO EXPIRATION!

Ladies, who could refuse that? Now that's a *great* coupon that would have me counting down the days to the start of that sale!

On the flip side, a coupon that said the following might be cut up rather than cut out:

Everything is 1% OFF

Regular-priced merchandise only

What a waste of paper! Is this a joke? This coupon stinks and is not worth the mailman's time to deliver it to you.

Good or bad, coupons are designed to accomplish three things:

1. Advertise for and give extra attention to its distributors.
2. Cause a reaction—the shopper either guards it or discards it.
3. Result in a purchase or a closed deal.

But what if the way we approach our singleness was marketed on a coupon? In dating, some of us discount ourselves or accept discounts from the men we "deal" with. But not all deals are ideal. So be careful how you advertise and what advertisements you are drawn to. Some coupons should be cut up versus cut out! Check out these examples.

90% OFF

ALL DAMAGED GOODS

Might look appealing at first glance, right? In retail shopping, you might be even tempted to sift through the damaged merchandise looking for the least damaged. Shoppers tend to do this because *damage* can vary. It could mean an item was used and returned, dropped in the store, or delivered with dings, dents, scratches, and scrapes—things that we may be willing to overlook because a 90 percent deduction is a deal that could override the damage. But caveat emptor, my dear. Buyer beware! Damaged goods are typically nonrefundable, don't carry a warranty, and are considered final sales.

Ladies, in dating, settling for damaged is dangerous. You can't assume that you can fix a man because the damage could definitely be irreparable. Putting a little tape or superglue on a vase might patch it up, but that won't fix a person with serious issues. In the long run, you might determine that someone who is damaged or broken should have been a deal breaker. So leave the damaged goods to the desperate shoppers. A whole you is definitely worth a whole him! We all have imperfections, a few dings and scrapes, a past and some mistakes. But *damaged* is different. Besides, you shouldn't enter a relationship knowing there are things about the other person that you want or need to fix or change. As in shopping, damaged daters are typically nonrefundable. They are considered "final sales" too because even when you let the relationship go, you still have lost some valuable things in the process; that is, the investment of your time, heart, and assets. Oftentimes, you cannot get these things back. Plus, a bad relationship may take some time to get over. So steer clear of the sales and clearance bins because only God can change or fix damaged men!

OBO

(Or Best Offer)

We have all seen those OBO signs. They are usually found on merchandise that the seller really needs to get rid of quickly. You might see OBO on a used or abused car, or on those not-so-gently-used items at a flea market or garage sale. When people see an item with an OBO sign stuck on it, they will purposely give a low offer, hoping it will be accepted by the seller as their best offer. While it may seem great to name your own price, OBO also requires the ability to negotiate. Unless you really know how to haggle, you could miss out on the best possible deal.

The same is true for negotiating deals in the dating world. So don't do it! Assign a high value to yourself, and stand by it. (For example, no sex*ing* without a ring.) Don't compromise. Don't settle for low offer just because you are ready to close the deal quickly. You don't want his OBO – a low offer disguised as his best offer. You want the offer that won't ask you to haggle and lower your values or standards. You will get the best possible deal (or guy) if you don't devalue yourself in order to attract a buyer who's looking for something cheap or something that he can talk down to little or nothing. When you realize you are worth something, you force others to either accept your terms or reject your offer and move on. Ladies, you are no OBO!

BUY ONE, GET ONE FREE
(BOGO)

This is probably the best deal in retail, hands down. You can't beat buying something and getting another something for free, which is why shoppers love this type of coupon. But have you ever considered that you might not actually need two of that something, or that the cost of the one item far outweighs the BOGO deal?

Yes, in some cases, BOGOs can be great, especially if they are truly a good deal. But getting BOGOs in dating doesn't entail free retail; they involve additional females. Relationship BOGOs happen when we bring extra people and their opinions into our relationships. Beloveds, we are notorious for babbling all our business to our buddies. But when you have prayed for Mr. Right, you believe that God has sent him, and you both are walking in a righteous relationship, God is the only one whose opinion matters. Mr. Right picked *you,* not the two or three or four of you. Pray for guidance in your relationship, read God's Word, and let Him give you advice. Sisters, don't bring a BOGO into your relationship, and don't date a man who comes with a BOGO!

Fine Print: I caution you with this coupon! There is nothing wrong with seeking wise counsel or the advice of a good friend, family member, mentor, or pastor. Often they can see what we tend to overlook, especially when we are in love. So please pay attention to those who love you and want the best for you. But God's Word gives the best advice on how to walk in a godly relationship. Plus, if you are truly seeking God's advice and approaching the relationship His way, He will reveal if Mr. Right is really Mr. Wrong.

ONE-DAY SALE

With Early-Bird Doorbusting Discounts

Whenever I hear that my favorite store is having a one-day early-bird sale, I mark my calendar and get up bright and early because the best deals happen first thing in the morning. I live for a good doorbuster! They are sporadic, for a limited time only, and they can give an additional discount on top of existing sales.

But, gals, one-day doorbusters don't work when dating. This sale is the equivalent to a one-night stand. You meet someone sporadically, and after knowing him for a limited time only, you discount yourself and allow him to bust down your (bedroom) door, getting your merchandise at a cheap, discounted price—that is, free! When dating, mark up your price to its full value and stop the doorbuster. You are worth far more than a "limited time only."

GIVEAWAY

With a Minimum Purchase

Ever had one of those coupons that will give you something for free or at a big discount with a minimum purchase?

For example, the coupon might read:

Receive a FREE tote bag with the minimum purchase of $50.00.

Gals, if a store can require a minimum purchase, shouldn't we? Yes, it's great to get free cute stuff, but the items still come at some cost.

So, ladies, brand yourselves with SASS—Set a Standard, Sis! Don't give anything else away without requiring a minimum—a minimum of a courtship, church wedding or courthouse ceremony, covenant, commitment, and circular band! When he makes the minimum purchase, let him have all the freebies he wants!

EXTREME COUPONING

A few of my friends have gotten into this new craze called *extreme couponing,* and they are serious about their Sunday papers and sales ads. They have couponing down to a science, and boy, do they save lots of money from searching for the discounts and accumulating lots of coupons. Once all their coupons are applied to their transaction, they end up getting their items for next to nothing.

Some of us have applied this same extreme method to our dating lives. We have discounted ourselves so much that we don't value ourselves, and neither does anyone else. Matter of fact, we've allowed others to treat us *extremely* poorly and use us so much that the resulting discounts make us feel we're not valuable or valued at all. More importantly, we've devalued ourselves so greatly we might as well advertise like a sales ad: "Cheap," "Free," "On Sale," "Discounted." By doing so, we begin to attract extreme couponers who are hunting for someone they can get for little to nothing.

Again, loves, stop letting others dictate your worth. Coupons definitely have value, but in dating, discounting and devaluing yourself is a NOGO! You are worth full price, plus interest. You come with no coupons, and you are no markdown. And you don't have to go to extremes to find love or to feel loved.

Ever notice that some coupons don't apply to certain items? Stores know that people will want those high-dollar items and brands, regardless of whether they're on sale or not. Consider yourself one of those "coupon does not apply" items. You are too good of a deal to be discounted. Once a great guy recognizes your value, this will result in three things:

1. He will recognize your worth (no coupon necessary).
2. He will guard and protect you and your heart.
3. He will get on one knee and close the deal.

God doesn't place you on the discount display or in the bargain basket, and neither should you or anyone else. So to go from coupon to couture, think DRESS!

D—Develop a biblically based mantra, and say it to yourself, write and post it everywhere, and memorize it to remind yourself of how valuable you really are. Remind yourself that God loves you and that you were created in His glorious image. The tongue speaks life and death. Speak life into yourself.

Here's my morning mantra:
Tiffany, you are the daughter of a King.
Regardless of what happens today, you can conquer anything.
So work that job like you were reporting to the Almighty.
Shine His light in your office and in your community.
You are fabulous and fierce and wonderfully made.
Get out of this bed, get jazzed up, and take control of this day.
Give your very best; don't let anyone or anybody make you stress.
Smile, encourage, and show the world that Tiffany Grant is blessed.
Make it a great day, you gorgeous gal!

R—Realize your worth by reading your Word. Open your Bible regularly and learn about who carefully handcrafted and created you. Pray that God will show you His purpose for your life so that you can concentrate on fulfilling that purpose. Learn about how much God values you, how much He loves you, and how much He wants to bless you. Instead of being fixated on the man and the details of who, when, what, where, and how, learn God's expectations of you so that you can exceed the expectations of the man that He has created for you.

E—Exude confidence. Jazz yourself up! But do it for you, even when you don't feel like it. Do what a bootleg purse does: fake it until you make it! Get into the habit of looking your best all the time. Trade in the warm-ups and ball caps for a cute do and jeans with bling. You can do it on a dime or a discount. Just remember to display the product without letting the tag hang out. Keep it *all* covered up in class. Leave something to the imagination. Don't walk around with the gift partially unwrapped! (I know you get my drift. Keep in mind that a great guy wants a confident, self-respecting woman.)

S—Save! Save! Save! Set some standards and don't settle for less. Wait and save for the right man *after* you get the wedding band. Save "it" for a man who shows you respect and values your inner and outer beauty. Don't compromise yourself and what you believe in just to stay in a substandard relationship. A man who truly wants to take you to the checkout counter will pay full price, and he won't mind waiting for and saving up for you and "it." We save up to buy everything of value in this world—a car, a house, vacations, an engagement ring, a wedding, college, retirement, etc. And yet we give our God-given bodies away for absolutely nothing! (More about this in a later chapter.)

S—Secure an accountability partner. Find a friend with similar interests, desires, and struggles and hold each other accountable. Pray for and encourage each other. Cheer each other on as you overcome life's twists and turns. Be intentional about this by checking in, on, and with her. Keep it real with her. When she starts shopping cheap, tell her! When she looks cheap, tell her! Most importantly, make sure your girl doesn't clip a coupon and place it across her chest. And allow her to do the same for you.

Chapter 4 Warranty

Read John 8: 1-11.

In John 8, a woman has devalued herself and stands in front of a crowd of men like a one-dollar item on display at the checkout aisle. This woman, labeled an adulteress, was caught having sex by the Pharisees. I can only imagine how humiliated and terrified she was. She was probably naked and sweaty, wrapped in a sheet, with men surrounding her holding rocks. But before the men could stone her, Christ stepped in and challenged them to examine their lives and their sins. He told them that if they were sinless, they could judge her and punish her. The men dropped those stones and left the scene. Jesus then showed compassion to the woman by telling her she was not condemned, and that she should leave her life of sin. As He has done for many of us, Jesus restored the woman's value when He saved her. While the Bible does not give an account of the rest of this woman's life, I'd bet my shopping budget that she never discounted herself again!

Chapter 4 Checkout

What I liked and learned while reading this chapter:

1.
2.
3.

What I want to live out and apply to my life going forward:

1.
2.
3.

Chapter 5

Smart Shoppers

Sistas, it is no secret that we love to shop, regardless of whether we have the money or not. Rarely can most of us turn down a good deal, bargain, or a must-have, even if we have to use credit, a "hot" check, or our very last stash of cash. If a woman sees any value in it, she will find a way to get it. The question for most of us is not if we shop. The question is how we shop.

Some of us are indecisive. Some of us know exactly what we're looking for before we even get to the store. Some of us like the "finer things in life." For others, cheap is king. Some of us appreciate the authentic while others buy bootleg. Some of us prefer boutique and one-of-a-kind; some like to shop in bargain basements on a dime. From Neiman Marcus to Walmart to the flea market, most of us enjoy shopping.

From low budget to no budget, we all fall into three major categories of shoppers:

1. Compulsive shoppers
2. Bargain shoppers
3. Smart shoppers

A *compulsive shopper* goes to a store knowing what she wants, but she ends up buying stuff she did not need or even intended to buy. Gimmicks get her attention. She falls prey to the red dots, red apples, gold stars, BOGO offers, clearance racks, percentage-off signs, the latest and greatest trends, and the hot new releases. These must-have offers cause her to lose her focus because she simply can't resist them. So she falls for the gimmick. And oftentimes, because it was a compulsive buy, she ends up regretting her purchase or returning it, after realizing she really couldn't afford it, really didn't need it, or that it really wasn't worth the money she spent or time she wasted on buying it.

A *bargain shopper* also goes to a store knowing what she wants—something for next to nothing. She goes straight to the clearance section. She is trying to find a jewel among the junk. She hunts the garage and estate sales too, and frequents resale shops. She loves to buy cheap and then brag about her discount purchases and how much they didn't cost. She's thrifty and will buy secondhand or gently used items, merchandise that's been picked over or even damaged because she thinks she can fix it and disguise its imperfections. She puts more value on the low price than on the item itself. It's important to note that when you look at some stuff on clearance, you can clearly see why it's 95 percent off. It's tacky, of poor quality, broken, or out of season. More importantly, when an item has been marked down so low that it's almost free, it's safe to assume that most people looked past it because they didn't see any value in it, regardless of its low price. But this shopper buys this bargain. And when she gets her bargain buy home, she adds it to the mounting collection of stuff that she got for next to nothing.

Disclaimer: Many of us consider ourselves bargain shoppers, so don't take offense at this analogy! When you reach the end of this chapter, if this bargain-shopper shoe fits, please take it off, take it back, or throw it out!

A *smart shopper* goes to a store knowing exactly what she wants and leaves the store with exactly what she intended to buy. Nothing more, nothing less. She might use a shopping list to help keep her focused and within her budget. She is patient and will shop around or save up for what she wants because she recognizes its value. She will travel far and wide until she finds it. She will not overextend herself or spend money on stuff she doesn't need or didn't plan to buy. She does not mind paying full price, if necessary. She can see past the gimmicks. She appreciates a good sale, but won't settle for something just because it's on display, cheap, or easy to come by.

Ladies, whether you realize it or not, we are all shoppers, from the shoes on our feet to the men that we meet. So, in the market of man-hunting, which kind of single shopper are you?

- ✓ Are you compulsive? Will any man do?

- ✓ Do you fall for the gimmicks that look good on the outside, even though there's no real value on the inside?
- ✓ Do you seem to end up with the ones who others have returned because they realized they really could not afford to waste any more time on him?
- ✓ Do you tend to look for bargains that end up costing you more than what he's worth?
- ✓ Do you give up your valuables just to close the deal?
- ✓ Do you have a tendency to rummage through damaged goods thinking you can fix him up or change him?
- ✓ Do your impulsive decisions lead you to compromise and bring home something that you didn't need and that just adds to your growing pile of baggage?
- ✓ Do you usually end up discovering that the must-have man should have stayed on the as-is shelf?
- ✓ Do you end up feeling cheap and undervalued once the transaction between the two of you is completed (and over)?

Disclaimer: I do not think or even want to imply that all men are dogs or intend to do us harm. However, some women undervalue themselves, leaving them vulnerable to acquiring cheap, damaged junk.

Ladies, we need to *learn to be smart shoppers*, from how we pick merchandise to how we determine the qualities we want in a man. We have to see a man as someone who will add value to who we already are and not just someone who can fill a hole in our lives. (No pun intended, but we need to stop that too until marriage!) He needs to be worthy of you. Like the smart shopper, we need to learn to wait on what we want and *save up for him*, versus spending (putting out or giving up) so much so quickly. When you save up for something special, it makes the purchase so worth the wait. So perhaps the lesson is that some of us need to stop shopping for them, pouncing on them, chasing them, begging them, throwing ourselves at them, giving stuff away to them, settling for any of them, and *wait* for God to send him to a complete, whole, confident, prepared, prayed-up, loving, supportive, submissive *you*!

Chapter 5 Warranty

Read Proverbs 18:22.

But wait! The Bible says (in the King James Version), "Whoso that findeth a wife findeth a good thing." I know, I know. It's 2015. These days, women shop till they drop when it comes to finding a man (which is why I wrote this book). And personally, I think it's okay for us ladies to look. But if a man is shopping for his wife, what type of shopper would you attract?

- ✓ Are you a bargain, cheap and easy to find?
- ✓ Are you a gimmick, placed in the center aisle with all her goods on display?
- ✓ Are you clearance? Would you be placed in a crowded sales bin with other items that have been picked over, used, marked down, and even a little damaged?

Or:

- ✓ Are you a smart buy that is worth all the time and effort that it took to find you?
- ✓ Would you be put on a high shelf with other valuables?
- ✓ Might you even be put under lock and key because your self-worth makes you extremely expensive and highly sought after?

Ladies, low self-esteem and lack of self-love, poor relationship choices, and past mistakes have caused some of us not only to settle for men of poor quality but also to discount ourselves. Some of us don't feel worthy of real love, so we put ourselves on sale and allow our relationships to damage our hearts, minds, and bodies, leaving us only 50 percent (or less) of who we should be. But God desires more from and for you, beloved. Know that God's loving grace restores your mistakes and can repair any damage and heartbreak. Strive to be the "good thing" that a great guy is looking to find.

Chapter 5 Checkout

What I liked and learned while reading this chapter:

1.
2.
3.

What I want to live out and apply to my life going forward:

1.
2.
3.

Chapter 6

Salesgals vs. Shopping Pals

Girlies, we all typically shop in one of two shopping scenarios:

1. With a shopping pal

2. With the "help" of a salesgal

There are definitely distinct differences between these experiences.

Scenario 1: Shopping with a Shopping Pal

Imagine it's a Saturday (after payday), and you finally have a free weekend. No cleaning necessary, no errands to run, no ministry meetings to attend, no Little League games, no hair appointments, no overtime to work. You've paid all the bills and you have a little left over to kill. So you pick up a friend and head to the mall, park in your favorite spot near your favorite store, and pray for favor on the sales rack.

The good thing about shopping with your shopping pal is that she knows you and your style. You are close girlfriends and always tell each other the truth. If it's too tight, you'll say, "Girl, that doesn't fit or look right." If it's outside the budget or costs too much, one of you will tell the other, "Look but don't touch." Your friend loves you and has your best interests at heart, even in the shopping cart. She knows what you like and don't like. She knows what complements you and what doesn't. She'll deter you from impulse buys, bad deals, and sale gimmicks. When you find a perfect buy, she celebrates the great price and cute merchandise as if it were her own. She is not competing with you to see who can spend the most or look the best. She's got your back when browsing the rack. More importantly, you are just as good of a shopping pal to her as she is to you.

Scenario 2: Shopping with "Help" from a Salesgal

Imagine that it's a Saturday (before payday) and your shopping pal was busy, so you opted to shop solo. Besides, your intention is to stop at the store, scan and select from the clearance section, and close the deal in less than an hour. But as soon as you set foot in her department, you meet up with the salesgal. Unlike your shopping pal, the salesgal is not your friend, although she seems friendly. She is there to help you and seems happy to do it.

She greets you with a smile and a "How may I assist you?" Part of you wants to say, "I'm doing fine on my own and want to be left alone," while another part wants to ask for help since you're shopping by yourself. Besides, she knows the whole store and exactly where stuff is located on the sales floor. So you smile back and share what you're shopping for: a new dress for Sunday service. The salesgal springs into action. Not only does she help you find a new outfit for Sunday, but she also suggests matching shoes that are the perfect size, with a purse, and jewelry to accessorize.

While shopping, the two of you begin to chat, laughing and talking about family and friends. She relates to you like a longtime girlfriend who knows what you like. She says all the right things and gives all the right compliments. Like, "Girl, that was made for your shape. It may cost a bit, but it sure looks great. Besides, I can offer you a new account with a low interest rate. You don't have to pay today. You can pay at a later date."

The salesgal is so smooth and so sly that she uses her sales pitch to push you right into the purchase pit—all for *her* benefit. You see—the salesgal doesn't care about you or your budget or the principal plus interest you will soon be paying outside of it. She doesn't have your best interest at heart. To you, she was a nice salesgal with good taste who helped you put together a great outfit (until you receive the new credit-card statement with that high credit-card rate). To her, you were a sale that she wanted to close, a quota that she needed to meet, and a shopper suckered into a new account with a beginning balance beyond her budget. As soon as you leave the store, she laughs about how a few smiles and slick talking earned her some sales.

Disclaimer: Refer back to chapter 1 for the disclaimer on salespeople. It still applies here! No offense, salesgals, but you and I both know that some of your coworkers (not you) are depicted above.

Sisters, are you wondering what salesgals and shopping pals have to do with living single or preparing for loving relationships?

Scenarios one and two illustrate how we as women interact with and treat one another. Unfortunately, we don't always love or even like each other. Too often, female relationships are plagued with cattiness, chatter, confusion, and competition. Like the salesgal, many of us have faux friendships that appear to be real but really are fake, fictitious, and phony.

Like the slick saleswoman, all of us have done one, some, or all of the following:

- smiled in a friend's face but talked about her behind her back
- sold her gimmicks by telling her what she wanted to hear versus what she needed to hear
- competed for the same merchandise (such as men, friends, or status) that she wanted
- spread her secrets faster than Sunday's sales ads

- failed to hold her accountable and help her to see her value
- held a clearance sign over her head, reminding her of all the times she discounted herself

It's time to stop settling for (or acting like) the faux (temporary, easily broken, and short-lived) friendships. It's time to invest in (or be the) real, authentic (long-term, strong, and well built) friends.

Loves, before we can truly be loving wives, I believe we have to master being loving friends to the wonderful women God puts in our lives.

I have heard some women say that they can't have too many female friendships because of "how women are." In my opinion, this is a tragedy, and it's time that we change that!

Divas, I believe that the devil seeks to cause drama and dysfunction in an effort to divide us. He knows that when women form unbreakable bonds, we are a unified force to be reckoned with. He also knows that division among us eventually becomes like a disease that eats away at our hearts and relationships and can result in the deaths of not only friendships but also dreams, families, churches, and businesses.

The Bible provides an example of two catty and competing women in the book of Genesis. The story of Rachel and Leah is full of drama that resulted in a divided family. Read Genesis 29–30 and jot down how this story parallels issues that women deal with today.

_____

_____

_____

_____

_____

The Bible describes Leah as "the sister with tender eyes," which was the politically correct way of saying that she was a little hard on the eyes. In the next verse, Rachel is described as "beautiful and well favored," which meant she was gorgeous and well liked. (Today's society also tries to use beauty and popularity to divide us.) So we can imagine there were constant comparisons made between the two sisters. Most people probably referred to Rachel as "the pretty one," while Leah was described as "having a great personality." Because of this, it's no surprise that Jacob fell hard for Rachel. So much so that he committed to working for her father for seven years to gain her hand in marriage. But the girls' father was sneaky, and he tricked Jacob into marrying his eldest daughter Leah, the eyesore, first. He then made Jacob work another seven years for Rachel. Rachel must have been one bad mama jama, because Jacob actually did it.

So after spending years being compared to each other, Rachel and Leah marry the same man. To add fuel to the fire, the Bible says that Jacob loved Rachel more than Leah, which most definitely would have become another area of contention between the women. Both loved him. Both were sleeping with him. Both competed for his attention, affection, and affirmation. (Over two thousand years later, women are still fighting over men like this!) Above all, both women competed to become the mother of his child. Leah bore babies left and right, while Rachel appeared to be barren. But Jacob still favored Rachel. So Leah continued having babies to win her husband's favor and to give her an edge over Rachel. As a result, Rachel, jealous of her fertile foe, invited her maids into her marriage, and they served as surrogates several times over. (Women are still compromising themselves to gain an edge over women whom they see as competition, or just to keep the attention of a man.) Can you imagine how intense the interaction between these two women was, full of arguments and insults, eye rolling and finger pointing, competition and division? Poor Jacob was in the middle. Talk about a love triangle!

How were Leah and Rachel more like salesgals than sisters?

- Both competed for the same man.
- Both were caught up in baby-mama drama, complete with using their kids as leverage.
- Both were consumed by jealousy, hatred, and division.

On the contrary, though, the Bible also shows an example of a faithful friendship between two women—Naomi and Ruth. Read the book of Ruth and jot down ways that it demonstrates the love and loyalty that women should share with someone they call friend.

_____

_____

_____

_____

_____

After the death of her husband and sons, Naomi was so hurt and soured that she named herself Mara, which means bitter. Despite her pain, she loved her daughters-in-law and urged them to return to their homes, rebuild their lives, and remarry. While one daughter-in-law left, Ruth remained with Naomi, refusing to leave her in a rut.

Naomi shared her wisdom with Ruth, teaching her what to wear, where to work, and how to win the heart and devotion of a well-respected man. Ruth's love for and loyalty to Naomi was ultimately rewarded by God when Boaz redeemed her and restored her joy. The beautiful bond between these two women was unbreakable and proved to be a blessing to them both and an example to all women.

How were Ruth and Naomi true shopping pals?

- Ruth was loyal enough to remain at Naomi's side during her depression.
- Both were loving and supportive of each other.

- Naomi shared life lessons with Ruth, who respect-fully listened, and those lessons eventually led her to true love.

While Ruth and Naomi illustrate the type of friends we should be, Rachel and Leah's relationship is a classic catty case, the type that we see in the media, in society, and too often in our own lives and circles of friends. I believe these relationships are described in God's Word because He wants us to use them as examples when framing our own friendships. Far too often, we let jealously, gossip, and men ruin what could be beautiful lifelong bonds.

Chapter 6 Warranty

Read Proverbs 18:24 and 27:17 and Ephesians 4:29.

Separate the salesgals from the shopping pals in your lives, ladies! Or stop being a salesgal yourself. Regardless of what some may say, great women need great women in their lives. All women are not catty and chatty. So support and share with your girlfriends. Love and lift each other up. Tell the truth and give your friends advice in love, even when it hurts. Hold each other accountable. Encourage one another to exceed goals, and be there to break and buffer any falls. Pray together through life's trials. Cheer for each other and celebrate life's victories. Besides, when you decide that you are in the market for Mr. Right, nothing is better for a single gal than having a good shopping pal. She loves you, knows what fits you, and has your best interests at heart, even in the shopping cart.

Chapter 6 Checkout

What I liked and learned while reading this chapter:

1.
2.
3.

What I want to live out and apply to my life going forward:

1.
2.
3.

**List the names of your girlfriends
who are super shopping pals!**

Chapter 7

Shopping Bags

Divas, it's Sunday afternoon (after church service) and you are ready for dinner. But you discover that the refrigerator is keeping two things cool: baking soda and a box of last night's leftovers. (Long sigh.) You know what this means. It's time to grab your shopping list, sales ads, and coupons and spend an hour or more at the grocery store. After strolling up and down all the aisles, snacking on samples, and comparing coupons and costs, you finally make it to the cashier and you hear that commonly asked question: "Paper or plastic?" Stores typically give you these two options, and you choose your bag type. Your groceries are bagged, and sometimes a nice bagger will even help you carry the load to your car. But once you get home, you have to unpack all your bags and then store them, recycle them, or throw them out.

Take a moment and think about which one you prefer, paper or plastic. Jot down a few reasons why you like one type of bag over the other.

_____

_____

_____

_____

_____

Check out some of the excess baggage (or problems) that can come when you choose to carry paper or plastic.

Plastic Bags:

➢ harmful to the environment (although they have become more "green" over the years)
➢ flimsy and have to be double bagged
➢ see-through and may not be good for a shopper wanting to hide the contents

➢ easily broken because they are not meant for heavy items

➢ collected but can quickly become clutter (Even though they are recyclable, most of us keep them around in case we need them. We then use and reuse them, sometimes for temporary storage of small amounts of junk or for trash. If not reused and discarded quickly, we can collect a gazillion of them.)

Paper Bags:

➢ sturdier, but they still tear when they are stuffed

➢ opaque and hard to see their contents, but that may not be good for a shopper who wants to identify quickly what's in her bags

➢ difficult to carry, especially those without handles

➢ if they have handles, the handles break off when the bags are too heavy

➢ collected but take up even more space than plastic bags (Even though they are also recyclable, most of us tend to store them longer than plastic bags because they can carry larger amounts.)

Personally, I don't like either option. I prefer the recyclable bag! While stores strategically place them near the checkout counters, recyclable bags are not offered for free. But to me, they are well worth the less than five bucks that you pay for them. Here's why:

Recyclable bags:

> ➤ environmentally friendly and require minimal storage
> ➤ made of sturdy but flexible fabric, and can hold more than the average paper or plastic bag
> ➤ some are see-through while others mask the contents with cute designs; variety of colors, shapes, sizes, etc.
> ➤ tend to last longer than paper or plastic bags
> ➤ can be used over and over again

Ladies, just like a shopper carries bags when shopping, we can sometimes carry baggage when we're shopping for a great guy. This excess baggage is often full of the hurt and disappointment that we've experienced in our lives. It can weigh us down and follow us from relationship to relationship. If we're not careful, the baggage we carry can multiply and overwhelm us, can rip and tear our worlds apart, adversely affecting our friendships and romantic relationships. Check out some of the types of bags that single gals (and married gals) carry into relationships.

Plastic-Bag Gals

Gals that carry plastic bags could be considered harmful to their own environment because they hang on to their hurt rather than recycling it; that is, letting go of the pain, guilt or relationships. They store their baggage in their hearts and minds and continue to put themselves in hurtful situations. Because they carry their past and pain with them, they have "bags" everywhere. These bags represent all sorts of things that these ladies have picked up, held on to, stored, and continue to carry. Contents (or excess baggage) like:

Baggage

Heartbreak   Fornication   Dreams deferred   Physical abuse   Betrayal
Death   Sin   Abandonment   Low self-esteem   Past hurts   Rejection   Lust
Sickness   Divorce   Financial hardships   Depression   Rape   Shame
Disappointments   Lies   Promiscuity   Break-ups   Distrust   Fear
Taken advantage of   Molestation   Poor self image   Abortion   Denial
Childhood scars   Unplanned pregnancy   Bullied
Adultery   Friendship fallouts   Neglect   Failures   Being cheated on
Addictions (alcohol/drug/sex/ pornography/masturbation, etc.)
Broken family   Absence of father (or mother)   Poverty   Mental abuse

You can see through these plastic bags, which means that women who carry them tend to be overly transparent. That makes them susceptible to someone who can see right through them and is looking to take advantage of them. Because plastic bags are flimsy, these women are not equipped to handle life's heavy disappointments. So they have difficulty coping, and they tend to break easily. They can't hold much and will gripe, gossip, complain, or cry on the shoulder of anyone who will listen. Girls who carry plastic bags hold onto things or people who they should have left at the curb long ago. Sometimes they revisit some of their just-in-case baggage (you know, the guy they keep around just in case they need someone one lonely night) over and over, instead of sending him to the trash (or recycle) bin where he might belong.

Paper-Bag Gals

Ladies who carry paper bags appear to have an advantage over the plastic-bag gals. Their bags hold more weight and provide more protection for the contents. The contents of plastic bags and paper bags are usually the same, as listed above. But paper-bag gals tend to use their hard exteriors and act as if the contents of their bags don't exist, especially since the outside world can't see what's inside. Paper-bag gals are sturdy and tough. They don't trust anyone, hold grudges, and tend to be stubborn and skeptical of good intentions. Since the bags' contents aren't easily visible, these ladies hold more and more in them, until they burst open or fly off the handle when the weight of the world gets too hard to carry. Women who carry paper bags often have an "I can handle it all by myself" mentality. They will hold things in and deal with them alone versus being more transparent and seeking help or counsel. Like the plastic-bag carriers, paper-bag gals still collect bags. The difference is that their baggage is bigger. For this reason, they hold on to more stuff and carry their heavier burdens longer, until they lose handle of the situation or issue.

Recyclable-Bag Gals

Girls who carry recyclable bags believe in being environmentally friendly. (I know what you're thinking, that plastic and paper can be recycled too. But recyclable bags cut down on the use of those bags altogether.) These women positively affect those around them, regardless of any personal burdens they might be carrying. Like the ladies who prefer paper or plastic bags, the women who use recyclable bags carry the same contents, as listed above. But they don't allow what they carry to break them so easily or cause them to fly off the handle. These ladies are cut from a different fabric, one that has the strength and flexibility to handle life's trials and tests. Because they carry bags made from recyclable materials, they can handle varying cycles and recycles in their lives by reusing prayer, God's Word, and His wise counsel, and by seeking the help and support of loved ones. Plus, they know when to be transparent and when they need to hold things in and handle them alone. Gals who prefer recyclable bags allow what they go through to color their lives, shape who they become, and contribute to their growth. Recyclable-bag gals have made a small investment in their bags. They often find that the bags are well worth it. Over time they come to know this bag so well that they understand what it can and cannot handle or carry. Despite toting difficult and heavy things, recyclable bags remain intact without any wear and tear (e.g., hang-ups, bad attitudes, misconceptions, assumptions, bitterness, inability to forgive, negativity, and resentment).

Ladies, at varying times in our lives, we've probably carried all three types of bags, not only in the grocery store but also in the dating world. I know I have! Relationships and how we handle all that they entail can create baggage in our lives. Over time, relationships can also result in some wear and tear. But when you let Him, God will not only equip you to carry life's heavy loads, He will carry them for you.

Chapter 7 Warranty

Read Psalm 55:22 and Psalm 68:19.

Remember the friendly bagger who helps you get your groceries to the car? Think of God as the friendly baggage carrier. When you find that your cart is overloaded with hurtful baggage, take comfort in knowing that God is always there to help you carry the load. But our Heavenly Father doesn't stop there. He'll even unpack the baggage, ensuring that you learn the lesson. Plus, He'll equip you with a flexible and strong bag that can handle what you carry, or He'll give you strength to throw out the excess baggage for good! You don't have to carry life's heavy loads by yourself. Cast those cares on God. He cares for you. He'll carry your bags!

Chapter 7 Checkout

What I liked and learned while reading this chapter:

    1.

    2.

    3.

What I want to live out and apply to my life going forward:

    1.

    2.

    3.

Chapter 8

Self-Checkout Lane

Lovelies, have you noticed the new trend that has emerged in retail and grocery stores?

Hint: it aims to put an end to the dreaded mile-long checkout line.

Yep, you guessed it. It's the self-checkout lane, the fast line for shoppers with few items in their shopping carts.

The concept of the self-checkout lane is great—*in theory.* Supposedly they save stores money in staffing costs through the use of automated "user-friendly" machines, while saving shoppers' time by not having to stand in long checkout lines. But in my experience, the self-checkout lane is sometimes user friendly, rarely fast, and almost always frustrating.

Check out some of the reasons I choose to check out with a cashier over self-checkout lanes:

✓ First, the self-checkout lane limits the number of items customers can check out; typically ten items or fewer. Sometimes when I go to the store, my intention is to grab a few items and go, but this never happens. So I get into a line with a cashier. How many times have you stood behind someone scanning twenty or more items in the self-checkout lane? Or done it yourself? (Don't you just hate the stares you get when you try to act like you don't have fifty items while the person behind you has just a carton of milk?)

✓ Most of the time, the scanners in the self-checkout lanes misread barcodes, coupons, and price tags. They tend to have a hard time recognizing specials and sale items. (Sometimes, the sucker does not work at all! Ugh!)

✓ The baggie carousel (that's what I call it) has that annoying automated voice that always reminds you to "Please place your items in the bag" after you've already placed them in the bag; or it says "Please remove your items from the bag" after you just removed them from the bag. (This drives me cray-cray-crazy.)

✓ Transactions in self-checkout lanes are timed, and you only have a millisecond to complete them! Okay, maybe longer than that, but it feels that way. I guess the self-checkout lanes don't understand that your coupons, cash, checks, or credit cards are at the bottom of your purse. The automated voice annoyingly asks if you need more time to complete your transaction. (When I press the *yes*,

I need more time option five times, you'd think the machine would catch a hint and quit asking me!)

✓ Above all, there is only one cashier to troubleshoot the many issues of all six self-checkout lanes. So when you run into one of the issues above, you are stuck waiting in line. (Isn't this the very thing you tried to avoid in the first place when you decided to stand in the fast lane?)

So how should we avoid the stress sometimes associated with shopping? It's simple, sisters! Be patient, stand in line, and wait until it's your turn to checkout.

Cashiers' lines are always longer because they handle the entire checkout for you. There are no limits on what you can purchase. The cashier scans the barcodes, coupons, and price tags. If his or her scanner does not work, it is fixed on the spot. There is also no time limit in the cashier's checkout lane. The cashier will help as long as you need him or her to because he or she is there to serve you. Plus, the cashier knows the store, so if you grab the wrong thing or need to add something, he or she knows exactly where to find it. The cashiers know the specials and promotions, and they will sometimes make suggestions to help save you money. You can miss these benefits when you are in a hurry and are unwilling to wait.

So why are we so quick to bypass the cashier's line? Ladies, that's simple too. We live in a microwave society and want everything quick, fast, and in a hurry. We don't want to wait patiently. We have to have stuff as soon as we realize we want it. We don't weigh options. In retail, we don't care about the cost of the dress, and we're not patient enough to see if it will go on sale. We want it now. We don't want to take time to prepare our food. We want it fast. So we buy fast (fatty) food because it's a quick selection and transaction. Waiting in line at the grocery store is no different. We want to get in and out. A quick transaction with little to no interaction!

Disclaimer: Dear Large Retail Store or Gigantic Grocery Chain, no offense, but this is my opinion based on my personal experience.

Oh, how this is analogous to our spiritual lives, ladies! We don't seek God in prayer or through His Word for the things that we desire. When we need to make decisions, we don't wait for His response. We want the answer quickly. And our dating lives are no different.

Loves, many of us are waiting in line for God to bring someone special into our lives; or at least we are trying to convince ourselves and others that we are waiting on God. But rather than waiting patiently, we jump into the singles self-checkout lane. In the process, we run into the same issues we experience at the retail or grocery store. Check these out.

The singles self-checkout lane should be limited to a few items too:

- Does he love the Lord?
- When you prayed about him, what did God say?
- Does he respect you?
- Is he willing to date and love you God's way?

But no, not us. We try to cram more than a few items into the basket and sneak them into the single's self-checkout lane. Items like:

- Is he six foot nine? Is he fine?
- Does he have a nice body and a firm behind?
- Does he have big hands and big feet?
- Does he have a nice smile and pretty teeth?
- Does he have money?
- Did he earn multiple degrees?
- Does he meet all one hundred of my other needs?

Girls, as in the grocery self-checkout lane, the single's self-checkout scanner is always off, especially when we try to checkout on our own. Without God's help, our scanner will misread every time. We will miss the warning signs we would have seen if we weren't rushing the transaction. We will even get annoyed by the little voice that tells us to remove our selection from our life, or to consider the option that may be less immediately appealing but is better for us.

The transactions in the singles self-checkout lane are timed transactions too, but we are the ones who set the timer. We try to check ourselves out quickly because we are impatient and don't want to wait on God. Many of us meet a man and decide that he is "the one" in two weeks, rushing him from the sales floor to the bedroom door.

Lucky for us singles who are out here shopping, this self-checkout lane also has a cashier who troubleshoots too. But He has to deal with the gazillion self-checkout lanes full of women who made the same hasty transaction and are experiencing errors, issues, mishaps, and mistakes, and now are waiting on Him to fix them. And while God is more than capable of fixing your issue, oftentimes He will make you wait on Him just to show you that you should have waited patiently from the beginning.

Chapter 8 Warranty

Read Matthew 6:33.

Ladies, as you pace the aisles, shopping for a great guy and weighing your options, know that God is *the* ultimate cashier. He knows what's on the market. He can assist you with locating exactly who you need and can give you the best recommendations based on His divine knowledge of you. God can address all concerns and answer all questions. And He is definitely able to troubleshoot your problems. So stay out of the self-checkout lane. Stand in line and patiently and prayerfully wait your turn, and spare yourself the headaches and heartaches associated with the "fast" lane. Matter of fact, before you even start shopping, seek Him first and watch how He adds to the shopping cart. (The healthy stuff, not the junk!)

Chapter 8 Checkout

What I liked and learned while reading this chapter:

1.
2.
3.

What I want to live out and apply to my life going forward:

1.
2.
3.

Chapter 9

Store Policies

Shoppers, ever notice how stores, companies, retailers, and manufacturers like to apply various ninety-day policies, provisions, or promises to their products and services? These rules are generally put in place to protect the company and the consumer. Some ensure satisfaction in a product or service, while others provide options in case the customer is dissatisfied.

Check out a few.

Return Policy

This policy provides parameters for customers who are dissatisfied with a product or service and want a refund. A return policy might read as follows:

Return Policy

*We will gladly accept the return
of your unwanted, unused, unworn, or unopened merchandise
and will offer you a full refund or an exchange at full value
within 90 days from the date of purchase.
Merchandise returned after 90 days will only be returned
in the form of a store credit at its present sales value.
We do not accept used, worn, or opened merchandise.*

Limited Warranty

This provision protects the customer by covering products and services for a limited time only, in case a replacement, repair, or refund is needed. A limited warranty may look like this:

Limited Warranty

*We proudly stand behind our products.
Your merchandise should have no damage or defect.
However, all of our products are protected by a
limited warranty that provides coverage for
up to 90 days after the date of purchase.
Within this warranty period, we will gladly
replace, repair, or refund damaged or defective products.*

Satisfaction Guarantee

This promise proclaims that the customer should be satisfied with a product or service. If the customer is not satisfied, the retailer or manufacturer will provide a refund. A sample of a satisfaction guarantee is below.

> ### *Satisfaction Guaranteed*
> *We guarantee that you will be 100% satisfied*
> *with your recent purchase.*
> *But if you buy it and try it*
> *and still don't like it, we will accept it back*
> *and give you a full refund*
> *within 90 days of purchase.*

Notice that each of these policies, provisions, or promises has specific terms and are time sensitive (typically within ninety days). Rarely will retailers and manufacturers make exceptions to these rules. These are standard industry practices, and most consumers clearly understand that. When and if we question or take issue with these policies, sales representatives are quick to say five words:

"I'm sorry. It's store policy."

So, sisters, what do a return policy, a limited warranty, and a satisfaction guarantee have to do with single gals like you and me?

I believe that singles, like retailers and manufacturers, should set parameters, provisions, and promises to ensure that we live out our single lives on specific terms that are time sensitive.

Society has recently attempted to create such a policy. Prominent authors, professional matchmakers, and popular self-proclaimed love gurus have begun promoting the idea that single people should wait at least ninety days before having sex with someone they are "seeing"—not to be confused with a committed-to or monogamous-with relationship—to give them an opportunity to get to know the person.

This ninety-day rule bothered me just a little bit, which is another reason why I wrote this book!

Disclaimer: Please know that I tentatively applaud writers who encourage women to adhere to the ninety-day rule, because it does give women who may have low or no standards some standards to follow.

Now don't get me wrong, girls, in a world where hook ups, one-night stands, casual sex, and not-all-the-way-just-oral sex are common occurrences on the first date or after the first few dates, setting a standard for singles to adhere to is long overdue. But why *just* ninety days?

While a store provides a refund within ninety days, or protects a purchase with a warranty for no more than ninety days, or guarantees a product for up to ninety days, shouldn't your "merchandise" be worth way more than that? Shouldn't you wait longer to decide if you should give your "product" away? Shouldn't your goods and services be covered (up) for more than ninety days? Aren't you worth more than a ninety-day satisfaction guarantee? What if he were to sample the goods within ninety days and then decide he was not satisfied and wanted a refund? Your value far exceeds that of a piece of jewelry, a set of tires, a flat screen TV, or a piece of furniture. You are worth way more than a ninety-day investment!

Shopping gals, it's time for us to set some new industry standards as singles. (Remember to have SASS.) Standards that we won't make exceptions to. Standards that we will enforce and adhere to. Standards that we will stand by. Here is a policy with standards that I propose for singles:

The Singles Policy

The Singles Policy

God used His best design when He created me. So, please know that I'm not low-budget or cheap. I'll never be a giveaway, on sale, on clearance, or an off-brand. But I'm well worth the wait and long-term investment of a ring on my hand. I require more than a 90-day policy. My love, loyalty, and lifelong commitment comes with an unlimited warranty. But read the fine print. I am abstinent. Saving myself for the love of my life. And, Mr. Customer, if you can accept these terms, you'll be blessed with a great gal and possibly a wonderful wife. If you can't adhere to

The Singles Policy and feel that my product won't meet your needs, take your business elsewhere because this Single Gal isn't FREE!

But I AM SATISFACTION GUARANTEED!

80

We must require that anyone checking out our retail respect these standards. If not, request a refund quickly (stop dating him immediately), put yourself back on the market, and take your shopping elsewhere!

Society says that you have to sample the goods or give something a try before you buy. But the Bible says the exact opposite. God's Word gives us a straightforward rule—*wait* until the wedding day. This provision protects us from the dissatisfaction that can ultimately lead to a refund of the relationship (that is, a breakup or divorce). This provision protects the partnership and seals it with an unlimited warranty. This promise guarantees satisfaction through the beauty of loving and respecting each other enough to save your bodies for an undefiled marital bed. If he can't respect your standards, respond with these five words:

"I'm sorry. It's my policy."

Extended Warranty

When consumers really value something, not only do they make the purchase, but they also invest in an extended warranty. Consumers make this often-expensive investment because they already know they want to keep the merchandise for a long time. They value the item so much that they make a lifelong investment at the time of purchase to ensure that the item is completely protected from any hurt, harm, or accidents. For example, when I purchased my car, I bought the extended warranty because

I wanted Favor (that's my car's name) covered from bumper to bumper, since I plan on keeping her for a long time.

You, my dear, should come with an extended warranty—an investment made at the beginning of the relationship that is designed to protect your valuables and maintain your value. What do I mean? When a great guy is getting to know the fabulous you, the respectful way you carry yourself should make him want to invest in you for the long run, not just an evening. He should want to respect you just as much as you respect you, so he won't ask you to compromise your values, and he'll respect the standards you've already set for yourself. He should realize from your initial interactions that you are extra special, someone who is definitely worth investing his time, his heart, and his money in. (Yes, I said *money*. I am old school and believe that more often than not, the man should pay for the date. I don't care about how much he makes. Plus, you don't have to be wined and dined. You can be practical and dine on a dime!) He should decide early on that you are worth protecting from any hurt or harm. He should recognize your worth and want to work hard to ensure that you know how valuable you are to him.

Plus, extended warranties are not refundable. Most people who purchase them have no intention of returning the item in the first place. A great guy should have no desire to return or replace a great gal like you!

But, sometimes, refunds, returns, and replacements are necessary.

Returning Unwanted Merchandise

When returning items, most of us fall into one of three categories:

1. *The Rapid Returner*
   This shopper wastes no time in returning her unwanted, unused, unworn, and unopened merchandise within the ninety days. She usually decides quickly that the items are unwanted and returns them within thirty days!

2. *The Reluctant Returner*
   This shopper places the items she knows she has to return in the trunk of her car in case she's in the vicinity of the store where she purchased them. But she forgets about them or cannot decide if she truly wants to return them. Or she loses the receipt because she hung on to the items too long. As a result, the reluctant returner reluctantly returns the item after the ninety-day cutoff.

3. *The Ratchet Returner*
   This shopper couldn't care less about the return policy. She has the audacity to open, wear, or use the item—with or without the tags attached—because she either bought the merchandise with the intent to use or wear it and return it, or she decided she didn't want it after she used or wore it. She then ratchetly attempts to return the items. (No offense, ladies, but you know that's a tad ratchet!)

Under category one, the rapid returner would receive a full refund because she adhered to the return policy and made her return within the ninety-day window.

Under category two, the reluctant returner would lose some of the value of the item because she returned it after the ninety days. Per the return policy, she would receive only the present value of the item, which might now be on sale, and as a credit she can use only at that store.

Under category three, the ratchet returner would lose *all* the value of the merchandise because its used or worn condition is a violation of the return policy. (Unless she successfully fooled the salesperson by skillfully wiping off the deodorant stains or ironing out the wrinkles. I worked in retail. I've seen it all!)

So come clean, sisters! Have you been a rapid returner, a reluctant returner, or a ratchet returner? Okay, okay. I've been all three at some point in my life. (Minus the deodorant stains!)

But in dating, making returns of an item you no longer want or need within ninety days is very important.

Imagine that you are in the market for Mr. Right. Rather than allowing God to lead the sales-and-search team, *you* assume the role and get stuck with Mr. Right Now. How do you know he's Mr. Right Now? He starts showing you why you've got to return him to the market *right now.* (You might return a man for several reasons: you have little in common with him, he has different expectations of where the relationship should go, he only wants to "open your purse," he displays aggressive and controlling tendencies, he makes a better male shopping pal than a Mr. Right, or he entertains several single shoppers at one time.)

Upon realizing that you need to reevaluate the relationship, you consider the three ways that you can return (or run from) Mr. Right Now:

1. *Rapidly Return Him*
    This shopper wastes no time in ending the relationship with Mr. Right Now after she rapidly realizes that the reasons why she has to return him outweigh the reasons why she might want to keep him. This shopper also puts Mr. Right Now back on the market *unused* and *unopened*— meaning, *no sex of any kind*. (More about this later.) Because of this, this shopper walks away with her *full* value.

2. *Reluctantly Return Him*
    This shopper hangs on to Mr. Right Now for far too long because she can't decide if she wants him or needs him. She eventually returns him reluctantly, but not before compromising her own purchase policy, which includes using his "merchandise" and opening up her "purse." In the process, she compromises her value and loses a lot of her time, part of her heart, and a little of her mind.

3. *Ratchetly Return Him*

This shopper uses Mr. Right Now right after she finds him. She wastes no time in devaluing herself by opening her purse. She uses him, and allows him to use and reuse her. (Some women will say that they are proud to be promiscuous and that society has a double standard about women and sexuality. I don't buy this! I believe that women who give their bodies to just about anybody are hurting or have been hurt. They are using sex to control a man, keep a man, or feel loved by a man because they lacked the love of a father or were hurt by men in their past.) This shopper may eventually attempt to return Mr. Right Now after she realizes that the value of her purse is nearing zero, or she may stay with him and become Mrs. Right Now. In some cases, the ratchet returner eventually realizes that Mr. Right Now (who's been kept way past the ninety-day window) should just be donated, given away, or thrown out.

Ladies, we have all shopped for Mr. Right, only to discover that he did not fit quite right. Perhaps he was too loose or too tight. Perhaps he proved too expensive or was a quick and cheap impulse buy. Perhaps we thought we had to have him at first sight, but then figured out that he really was not Mr. Right. Regardless of the reason, we've all been in those situations where we knew we needed to make a return rapidly. With a little prayer and improved shopping choices, the reluctant and ratchet returners' value and self-worth can be fully restored, especially if they learn from the loss and remember to make any future returns within the ninety-day terms and to always adhere to the singles policy.

Chapter 9 Warranty

Read Matthew 1:25 and Hebrews 13:4.

Society says that a ninety-day policy gives you adequate time to get to know your potential partner before having sex. Did you know that in the Bible, "getting to know" means lying with your spouse for the *first* time *after* the wedding? Perhaps by extending this ninety-day policy, you will fully cover your relationship with love and respect, versus basing it on lust and sex. You will protect your heart from the hurt that can plague a relationship that is outside of God's instruction. Ultimately, you will guarantee your own satisfaction when a loving man decides to extend a lifetime warranty to you by making you his wife.

Chapter 9 Checkout

What I liked and learned while reading this chapter:

1.
2.
3.

What I want to live out and apply to my life going forward:

1.
2.
3.

Chapter 10

Online Shopping

Beloveds, one of the biggest shopping days across the country is the Monday after Thanksgiving—Cyber Monday. On Cyber Monday, computers across the country crash continuously and operate at a snail's pace because of the overwhelming overload of online shoppers racing to click on the hottest deals, best bargains, and lowest prices of the holiday season.

Aside from Cyber Monday, shopping online has become a popular option for today's shoppers. Check out several reasons why:

- You can shop from the comfort of your home, on the couch in your comfy clothes.
- Shopping online requires very little effort—a click on the computer or cell phone or tablet, or any other techy option.

- You avoid driving to stores and waiting in long lines.
- The World Wide Web happily accepts several forms of payment: check, credit, or debit.
- Shopping online can be done solo, with no need for communication or interaction with salesmen and their sales pitches.

Online shopping is a convenient way to browse for and buy the best deal based on your specified search criteria.

Well, girls, we now have the option of "shopping" for other singles on the Internet too. It's called online dating. It offers similar benefits to online shopping:

- Most users browse online dating sites from the comforts of their homes, on the couch in comfy clothes.

- Online dating requires very little effort—a click on the computer or cell phone or tablet, or any other techy option.
- You can avoid going places to meet people the old-fashioned way—in person.
- Dating sites on the World Wide Web happily accept all kinds. No background checks, credit checks, ID verification, criminal histories, psychiatric evaluations, etc.
- If online daters choose to, they can simply scroll through their dating options without any voice communication or face-to-face interaction.

Online dating is a convenient way to browse for and locate a potential mate based on your specified search criteria.

Disclaimer: I am not bashing online dating. In this day and age, we all know couples who met in cyberspace and fell in love. We live in such a high-tech society that social media has become cupid to many couples looking for connections via their computers. However, this chapter is based on my experiences with online dating, and that of my girlfriends, which have been interesting to say the least. So I don't discourage digital dating, but I do caution you to be careful. Don't fall for an eyeful who might be selling a bunch of bull. And, as in all things, remain prayerful.

Now it's time for me to get a little personal. Several friends suggested that I consider online dating. So after much contemplation, I created a personal profile on a few popular sites just to see what all the hoopla was about. I must say, I went from few options in my dating pool to options from sea to shining sea. There were thousands of men in my area looking to link up with a special lady. In the beginning, I wondered why I hadn't logged on and looked online sooner. But then, after a few weeks, I discovered why online dating might not be for me.

Fine Print: I use the term *might* because I may log on and look again.

While chatting online, I discovered that cyberspace is filled with an interesting cast of characters. Several of my girlfriends can attest to the following characterizations. So can you, if you've ever decided it was your time and dipped your toe in the pond, attempted to harmonize with a special him, tried to mingle or find your match, or hoped that cupid's arrow would come through your computer screen. (Hint: you might catch this if you've ever fished or surfed for singles.)

Cyberspace characters can (and guys, gals do these things too!):

- misrepresent themselves with old, outdated photos (e.g., posting past pics of a buff body versus posting present pics of the battle of the bulge);
- remain anonymous by using fake names unrelated to their real identities (e.g., SexyDaddy4U);
- avoid contact by limiting communication to a computer screen (e.g., messaging, posts, and texts have replaced long phone calls and long walks filled with talks);

- mislead, lie, or just make up their life stories as they go along (e.g., catphishing, an online romance scam, has become popular on social media);
- connect and disconnect at any time, regardless of any connection you think you've made (e.g., someone logs off and never logs back on);
- sift through or search according to specifications (e.g., for certain "assets" showcased in photos and the perceived likelihood that the poster would be willing to share his or her assets);
- communicate with multiple users at the same time (i.e., play the online field);
- claim to be single while actually being in committed relationships or in holey (as opposed to holy) matrimony (a.k.a. cyber cheaters);
- be thieves seeking to snatch your "purse" (some are only looking to hook up); or
- be actual criminals looking to commit real crimes. (We have all heard of rapists, murderers, and thieves lurking behind their computer screens.)

Disclaimer: I met some seemingly nice men online who seemed to have good intentions and who were equally interested in meeting a good woman. Not all fit the characteristics described above. So, fellas, don't be offended. I *might* not be talking about you.

Ladies, as with retail shopping online, you have to be cautious and careful when dating online! Not everyone online is honest husband material looking for a loving, committed relationship with a lifelong partner. Some folks are cyber crooks with ill intentions. It's like shopping on the Internet and being careful with your passwords and personal information. Online daters should also use caution with whom they exchange words and personal information. Ultimately, cyberspace characters can expose you to a computer love virus that can break your heart, deceive you, and destroy you if you don't detect him early. So you must put up safeguards—some antivirus software, so to speak—to protect yourself.

By now, you know I'm a list maker. (Except for *t-He* list; I'm letting God write that one.) So here goes another one:

Antivirus Tips for Dating Online

- Use a respectful head-shot photo and see how many are interested when your assets are not on display in your profile pics. (Stop taking the legs-open, cleavage-out, or look-at-my-butt pics please. You say you want respect, so respect yourself!)
- Use a dignified, anonymous user name to protect your identity. (You can exchange real names later.)
- Don't be so quick to exchange phone numbers. Chat online for a few weeks (maybe less than ninety days) before giving up your personal info. (Let personal info be the only thing you eventually give up!)
- Ask probing questions to see if you can detect a fictional from a factual life story. (It's okay to be inquisitive on the Internet.) Probing questions like, Ever been married? What church do you

attend? How old are your kids? Tell me a little about your mother. How was work?

- Disconnect if you feel disrespected or feel that his motives are devious. (Some online daters quickly reveal their intentions and what they're really interested in. If they don't line up with your intentions, delete!)

- Ask him what he's looking for online and why he's looking for a connection in cyberspace. (Again, inquiries on the Internet are important.)

- Communicate with multiple users, but be honest and clear about your intentions and ask that they do the same. (Players play the online field too.)

- Do not entertain anyone who indicates he is married but unhappy or is in a situation that's "complicated." Run from users in relationships! (Disconnect and delete immediately.)

- The first face-to-face date should be in a public place *after* you have moved from chatting online to conversing on the phone. Tell a friend where you're going, what time you're going, and who you are going with. Snap a pic of him and his license plate and send it to your girlfriends for safekeeping, in case you come up missing. No nightcaps at his place. Be smart! Be safe!

Fine Print: All the above rules should apply to dating in general, both the old-fashioned way and the online way!

Chapter 10 Warranty

Read Ephesians 5:15–17.

God wants us to be wise, especially because we are living in evil times. While social media gives us creative ways to meet other singles, it also gives people with ill intentions a creative place to play. So don't be foolish. Be a www.www.com woman: a Woman With Wisdom on the World Wide Web when Communicating Online with Men! Maintain your integrity and browse for a man who appears to be doing the same. When you meet him in person, get to know him and verify his ID. Make sure he is who he proclaimed to be. Understand that God's will is for you to connect with someone special, but disconnect quickly if you detect fraud or a virus!

Chapter 10 Checkout

What I liked and learned while reading this chapter:

1.
2.
3.

What I want to live out and apply to my life going forward:

1.
2.
3.

Chapter 11

On Layaway—Tiff's Testimony

Ladies, when I was young, my parents put *everything* on layaway—Christmas gifts, birthday presents, school clothes, etc. Boy, did we hate it! It was like looking through a window at everything you wanted without being able to touch it for six to nine months. Talk about torture! But layaway has its benefits.

For those of you who don't know what layaway is, let me break it down for you. Some stores offer customers, even to this day, the option to pay on layaway. Layaway allows you to pick out stuff and then put it aside with the assurance that it is yours, while you make payments on it until it is completely paid for. You can't get anything out of layaway before paying off the balance that is due. Matter of fact, you can't look at it, touch it, or take it home and use it unless it is paid for in full!

Layaway was a great concept for my family because it allowed my mom and dad to get what we needed with time to pay for it. Plus, our new school clothes remained untouched, unworn, and undamaged until school started. Chris and I really looked forward to those items. We made plans for them and counted down the days to when my folks would make that final payment. And when the items came out of layaway, they were appreciated, used, reused, and used some more!

Layaway taught me a valuable lesson: *that valuables (defined as a things of great worth) are worth waiting for.*

Well, girls, at sixteen I decided to put myself on a layaway plan, meaning that I would wait until marriage to get *lay-d* or to give anything *away*. I put myself and my merchandise on hold as I waited for a special someone to come along and pay for me in full. Guess what? I'm still holding out for Mr. Right, making me a thirty-seven-year-old virgin. (No, I'm not kidding! And yes, I'm proud to be the big *V.*)

Trust me: this decision has not been easy. I have been tempted time and time again. And again and again. I have been in situations when I have had to walk away, knowing that I wanted to do *it* at that moment. But with God's help and His divine intervention, I have stayed committed.

When I tell people that I am a virgin, their reactions vary. Some laugh. Some assume something is wrong with me. Some people are shocked, and some don't believe me. Some assume it's been a difficult decision, while others feel sorry for me because they think I'm "missing out." Some think it's old-fashioned; some have said it's admirable. Most of them are right. My decision has been tough. I do have old-school values. If I'm completely honest, at times I have felt like I am missing out and that something's wrong with me. But the decision to hold off on sex until marriage is an admirable one, and my hope and prayer is that my testimony will encourage and empower others to remain virginal until marriage, or to recommit themselves to a life of celibacy until they get married.

A life without premarital sex has allowed me to have so many freedoms, such as

- freedom from flings that amounted to nothing (not even a promise ring);
- freedom from the difficulty of having children out of wedlock or rushing weddings due to getting knocked up;
- freedom from the pain of unplanned pregnancy, miscarriage, or abortion;

- freedom from STDs;
- freedom from the temporary insanity that can arise when a woman realizes she's been used; and
- freedom from the guilt and hurt associated with giving your valuables to someone who later discarded them.

But I have to keep it real. This walk has not been easy. My layaway plan has been plagued by the following:

➢ short-term relationships with men who could not understand my commitment, conviction, and chastity

➢ the why-nots, the what-ifs, the whens, and the will-I-evers (I love him, so why not? I'm temporarily caught up in him, so what if? When will I meet Mr. Right [because I am really ready right now]? Will I ever give it up, or should I just hang it up?)

➢ the unknowns (These led me to learn all that I could about sex without actually doing it. As a teen, I read teen romance books. As a college student, I collected those steamy adult novels. Then I moved up to watching cable TV after ten o'clock at night. Then I graduated to taking sneak peeks at adult films. Before I knew it, I was thinking about having sex more than people who were actually having sex.)

➢ society's obsession with sex (Sex is everywhere you turn—music, commercials, billboards, radio, the Internet. So even when I wanted to shake the thoughts, they were in my face, shaking at me.)

The Bible says that "it is better to marry than to burn" (1 Cor. 7:9). Well, ladies, I was burning with the fire and desire! At thirty-seven, I still have to be careful about what I listen to and what I watch in order to stay focused on fulfilling God's plan for my life. I still desire a man, marriage, and motherhood. I look forward to the day when God blesses me with Mr. Right. But I also realize that when you trust God and wait on Him, He will push you right past that peer pressure and burning passion - straight into your purpose and in line with the path He has paved for your life. Waiting on God has given me clarity that enables me to go for every goal, chase every dream, and breathe life into every creative thought that He put into me. Now don't get me wrong. I look forward to my man and my undefiled marital bed, *but* I am willing to stay on layaway until God brings us together.

The choice to wait has blessed my life and has allowed me, prayerfully, to bless your life with this book.

Gals, this shopper has been in the market for a good, God-centered relationship for quite some time, but my valuables are under lock and key, and my purse is zipped—*temporarily.* When Mr. Right picks me out, puts me at his side, and pays for me in full (through dating God's way and putting a ring on it), this merchandise will be appreciated, used, reused, and used some more!

Disclaimer: Ladies, it's never too late to put yourself on layaway. You are worth the wait! Lock your valuables up until they are completely paid for.

Chapter 11 Warranty

Read Jeremiah 29:11 and 1 Corinthians 7:32.

Ladies, while I desire a happily ever after, with the love, marriage, and baby carriage, I take comfort in knowing that God knew my future way before my parents fell in love. I also know that He has big plans for my life, and all He requires is that I work purposely for Him while I wait patiently on Him. Girls, that is exactly what I am committed to doing.

Chapter 11 Checkout

What I liked and learned while reading this chapter:

1.
2.
3.

What I want to live out and apply to my life going forward:

1.
2.
3.

Chapter 12

444 Favs from Tiff's Fabulous Friends

Friends, many companies arrange for focus groups to preview their products or ideas. Comprised of the demographic that the company is targeting, these focus groups help to predict how shoppers will respond to a product. Focus groups provide the opportunity for companies to get open and honest feedback that they can use to improve their products before introducing them to all of us.

On January 31, 2014, I invited twenty wonderful women to participate in a focus group of sorts: to preview *The Single Gal's Guide to Shopping for a Great Guy*. These women were a beautiful blend of ages and ethnicity, with varying backgrounds and life experiences. Half of them were single, and half of them were married. Some were mothers, and some had no children. I wanted to introduce *The Single Gal's Guide* to this small group of friends to get their open and honest opinions, since all of these lovely ladies had "shopped" as singles, and had shared similar desires and disappointments while dating. Little did I know that this night would become much more than a sneak peek. The feedback, encouragement, prayers, and support from these phenomenal women proved invaluable to me as I worked to complete this book.

Toward the end of our time together, I broke the ladies into three groups and asked them to discuss and list their favorite Bible verses—ones that provided them with encouragement, instruction, comfort, correction, strength, and assurance. I'd like to share the more than four hundred of my fabulous friends' favorite verses with you. Please make it a goal to read each and every verse. Jot down what you take from them. Meditate and memorize the verses that become your favorites. Because I love lists, I listed each verse so that you can highlight them or check them off as you read them.

1.	2 Chronicles 20:15	35.	1 Corinthians 7:28
2.	Colossians 3:18	36.	1 Corinthians 7:29
3.	1 Corinthians 6:9	37.	1 Corinthians 7:30
4.	1 Corinthians 6:10	38.	1 Corinthians 7:31
5.	1 Corinthians 6:18	39.	1 Corinthians 7:32
6.	1 Corinthians 6:19	40.	1 Corinthians 7:33
7.	1 Corinthians 6:20	41.	1 Corinthians 7:34
8.	1 Corinthians 7:1	42.	1 Corinthians 7:35
9.	1 Corinthians 7:2	43.	1 Corinthians 7:36
10.	1 Corinthians 7:3	44.	1 Corinthians 7:37
11.	1 Corinthians 7:4	45.	1 Corinthians 7:38
12.	1 Corinthians 7:5	46.	1 Corinthians 7:39
13.	1 Corinthians 7:6	47.	1 Corinthians 7:40
14.	1 Corinthians 7:7	48.	1 Corinthians 13:4
15.	1 Corinthians 7:8	49.	1 Corinthians 13:5
16.	1 Corinthians 7:9	50.	1 Corinthians 13:6
17.	1 Corinthians 7:10	51.	1 Corinthians 13:7
18.	1 Corinthians 7:11	52.	1 Corinthians 13:8
19.	1 Corinthians 7:12	53.	2 Corinthians 2:4
20.	1 Corinthians 7:13	54.	2 Corinthians 6:14
21.	1 Corinthians 7:14	55.	2 Corinthians 10:3
22.	1 Corinthians 7:15	56.	2 Corinthians 10:4
23.	1 Corinthians 7:16	57.	2 Corinthians 10:5
24.	1 Corinthians 7:17	58.	2 Corinthians 12:9
25.	1 Corinthians 7:18	59.	Ephesians 4:32
26.	1 Corinthians 7:19	60.	Ephesians 5:3
27.	1 Corinthians 7:20	61.	Ephesians 5:4
28.	1 Corinthians 7:21	62.	Ephesians 5:5
29.	1 Corinthians 7:22	63.	Ephesians 5:6
30.	1 Corinthians 7:23	64.	Ephesians 5:7
31.	1 Corinthians 7:24	65.	Ephesians 5:22
32.	1 Corinthians 7:25	66.	Ephesians 5:23
33.	1 Corinthians 7:26	67.	Esther 1:1
34.	1 Corinthians 7:27	68.	Esther 1:2

69. Esther 1:3
70. Esther 1:4
71. Esther 1:5
72. Esther 1:6
73. Esther 1:7
74. Esther 1:8
75. Esther 1:9
76. Esther 1:10
77. Esther 1:11
78. Esther 1:12
79. Esther 1:13
80. Esther 1:14
81. Esther 1:15
82. Esther 1:16
83. Esther 1:17
84. Esther 1:18
85. Esther 1:19
86. Esther 1:20
87. Esther 1:21
88. Esther 1:22
89. Esther 2:1
90. Esther 2:2
91. Esther 2:3
92. Esther 2:4
93. Esther 2:5
94. Esther 2:6
95. Esther 2:7
96. Esther 2:8
97. Esther 2:9
98. Esther 2:10
99. Esther 2:11
100. Esther 2:12
101. Esther 2:13
102. Esther 2:14
103. Esther 2:15
104. Esther 2:16
105. Esther 2:17
106. Esther 2:18
107. Esther 2:19
108. Esther 2:20
109. Esther 2:21
110. Esther 2:22
111. Esther 2:23
112. Esther 3:1
113. Esther 3:2
114. Esther 3:3
115. Esther 3:4
116. Esther 3:5
117. Esther 3:6
118. Esther 3:7
119. Esther 3:8
120. Esther 3:9
121. Esther 3:10
122. Esther 3:11
123. Esther 3:12
124. Esther 3:13
125. Esther 3:14
126. Esther 3:15
127. Esther 4:1
128. Esther 4:2
129. Esther 4:3
130. Esther 4:4
131. Esther 4:5
132. Esther 4:6
133. Esther 4:7
134. Esther 4:8
135. Esther 4:9
136. Esther 4:10

137. Esther 4:11
138. Esther 4:12
139. Esther 4:13
140. Esther 4:14
141. Esther 4:15
142. Esther 4:16
143. Esther 4:17
144. Esther 5:1
145. Esther 5:2
146. Esther 5:3
147. Esther 5:4
148. Esther 5:5
149. Esther 5:6
150. Esther 5:7
151. Esther 5:8
152. Esther 5:9
153. Esther 5:10
154. Esther 5:11
155. Esther 5:12
156. Esther 5:13
157. Esther 5:14
158. Esther 6:1
159. Esther 6:2
160. Esther 6:3
161. Esther 6:4
162. Esther 6:5
163. Esther 6:6
164. Esther 6:7
165. Esther 6:8
166. Esther 6:9
167. Esther 6:10
168. Esther 6:11
169. Esther 6:12
170. Esther 6:13
171. Esther 6:14
172. Esther 7:1
173. Esther 7:2
174. Esther 7:3
175. Esther 7:4
176. Esther 7:5
177. Esther 7:6
178. Esther 7:7
179. Esther 7:8
180. Esther 7:9
181. Esther 7:10
182. Esther 8:1
183. Esther 8:2
184. Esther 8:3
185. Esther 8:4
186. Esther 8:5
187. Esther 8:6
188. Esther 8:7
189. Esther 8:8
190. Esther 8:9
191. Esther 8:10
192. Esther 8:11
193. Esther 8:12
194. Esther 8:13
195. Esther 8:14
196. Esther 8:15
197. Esther 8:16
198. Esther 8:17
199. Esther 9:1
200. Esther 9:2
201. Esther 9:3
202. Esther 9:4
203. Esther 9:5
204. Esther 9:6

205. Esther 9:7
206. Esther 9:8
207. Esther 9:9
208. Esther 9:10
209. Esther 9:11
210. Esther 9:12
211. Esther 9:13
212. Esther 9:14
213. Esther 9:15
214. Esther 9:16
215. Esther 9:17
216. Esther 9:18
217. Esther 9:19
218. Esther 9:20
219. Esther 9:21
220. Esther 9:22
221. Esther 9:23
222. Esther 9:24
223. Esther 9:25
224. Esther 9:26
225. Esther 9:27
226. Esther 9:28
227. Esther 9:29
228. Esther 9:30
229. Esther 9:31
230. Esther 9:32
231. Esther 10:1
232. Esther 10:2
233. Esther 10:3
234. Galatians 5:16
235. Galatians 5:17
236. Galatians 5:18
237. Galatians 5:19
238. Galatians 5:20
239. Galatians 5:21
240. Galatians 6:9
241. Genesis 2:18
242. Genesis 2:22
243. Genesis 2:23
244. Genesis 2:24
245. Hebrews 13:4
246. Isaiah 40:29
247. Isaiah 40:30
248. Isaiah 40:31
249. Isaiah 41:10
250. James 1:2
251. James 1:3
252. James 1:4
253. James 1:5
254. James 1:19
255. Jeremiah 1:5
256. Jeremiah 29:11
257. John 4:7
258. John 4:8
259. John 4:9
260. John 4:10
261. John 4:11
262. John 4:12
263. John 4:13
264. John 4:14
265. John 4:15
266. John 4:16
267. John 4:17
268. John 4:18
269. John 4:19
270. John 4:20
271. John 4:21
272. John 4:22

273. John 4:23
274. John 4:24
275. John 4:25
276. John 4:26
277. John 4:27
278. John 4:28
279. John 4:29
280. John 4:30
281. John 11:35
282. John 14:27
283. 1 John 4:7
284. 1 John 4:8
285. Mark 11:24
286. Matthew 6:24
287. Matthew 6:25
288. Matthew 6:33
289. Matthew 11:28
290. Matthew 11:29
291. Matthew 19:4
292. Matthew 19:5
293. Matthew 19:6
294. 1 Peter 3:3
295. 1 Peter 3:4
296. 1 Peter 5:7
297. Philippians 4:8
298. Philippians 4:13
299. Proverbs 3:5
300. Proverbs 3:6
301. Proverbs 3:7
302. Proverbs 3:8
303. Proverbs 3:13
304. Proverbs 3:14
305. Proverbs 3:15
306. Proverbs 3:16
307. Proverbs 3:17
308. Proverbs 3:18
309. Proverbs 5:1
310. Proverbs 5:2
311. Proverbs 5:3
312. Proverbs 5:4
313. Proverbs 5:5
314. Proverbs 5:6
315. Proverbs 5:7
316. Proverbs 5:8
317. Proverbs 5:9
318. Proverbs 5:10
319. Proverbs 5:11
320. Proverbs 5:12
321. Proverbs 5:13
322. Proverbs 5:14
323. Proverbs 5:15
324. Proverbs 5:16
325. Proverbs 5:17
326. Proverbs 5:18
327. Proverbs 5:19
328. Proverbs 5:20
329. Proverbs 5:21
330. Proverbs 5:22
331. Proverbs 5:23
332. Proverbs 6:16
333. Proverbs 6:17
334. Proverbs 6:18
335. Proverbs 6:19
336. Proverbs 10:1
337. Proverbs 10:2
338. Proverbs 10:3
339. Proverbs 10:4
340. Proverbs 10:5

341. Proverbs 10:6
342. Proverbs 10:7
343. Proverbs 10:8
344. Proverbs 10:9
345. Proverbs 10:10
346. Proverbs 10:11
347. Proverbs 10:12
348. Proverbs 10:13
349. Proverbs 10:14
350. Proverbs 10:15
351. Proverbs 10:16
352. Proverbs 10:17
353. Proverbs 10:18
354. Proverbs 10:19
355. Proverbs 10:20
356. Proverbs 10:21
357. Proverbs 10:22
358. Proverbs 10:23
359. Proverbs 10:24
360. Proverbs 10:25
361. Proverbs 10:26
362. Proverbs 10:27
363. Proverbs 10:28
364. Proverbs 10:29
365. Proverbs 10:30
366. Proverbs 10:31
367. Proverbs 10:32
368. Proverbs 11:13
369. Proverbs 13:20
370. Proverbs 16:3
371. Proverbs 16:18
372. Proverbs 18:22
373. Proverbs 18:24
374. Proverbs 20:19
375. Proverbs 21:9
376. Proverbs 27:17
377. Proverbs 31:10
378. Proverbs 31:11
379. Proverbs 31:12
380. Proverbs 31:13
381. Proverbs 31:14
382. Proverbs 31:15
383. Proverbs 31:16
384. Proverbs 31:17
385. Proverbs 31:18
386. Proverbs 31:19
387. Proverbs 31:20
388. Proverbs 31:21
389. Proverbs 31:22
390. Proverbs 31:23
391. Proverbs 31:24
392. Proverbs 31:25
393. Proverbs 31:26
394. Proverbs 31:27
395. Proverbs 31:28
396. Proverbs 31:29
397. Proverbs 31:30
398. Proverbs 31:31
399. Proverbs 37:8
400. Proverbs 37:9
401. Psalm 1:1
402. Psalm 1:2
403. Psalm 1:3
404. Psalm 24:1
405. Psalm 24:2
406. Psalm 24:3
407. Psalm 24:4
408. Psalm 24:5

409. Psalm 24:6
410. Psalm 24:7
411. Psalm 24:8
412. Psalm 24:9
413. Psalm 24:10
414. Psalm 27:1
415. Psalm 34:8
416. Psalm 34:13
417. Psalm 37:4
418. Psalm 91:1
419. Psalm 91:2
420. Psalm 139:14
421. Romans 2:1
422. Romans 3:23
423. Romans 8:1
424. Romans 8:28
425. Romans 8:37
426. Romans 8:38
427. Romans 8:39
428. Romans 12:1
429. Romans 12:2
430. Romans 12:3
431. Song of Solomon 1:1
432. Song of Solomon 1:2
433. Song of Solomon 1:3
434. Song of Solomon 1:4
435. Song of Solomon 1:5
436. Song of Solomon 1:6
437. Song of Solomon 1:15
438. Song of Solomon 1:16
439. Song of Solomon 1:17
440. Song of Solomon 4:7
441. 1 Thessalonians 4:3
442. 1 Thessalonians 4:4
443. 1 Thessalonians 4:5
444. 2 Timothy 1:7

I pray that all the Bible verses above encourage you, empower you, and enlighten you! But please know that the Bible has so much more than even these four-hundred-plus verses. Everything you need for every situation you are in, every trial that you go through, or anything you need an answer to can be found in the Word of God. While *The Single Gal's Guide* gives some guidance, the Bible is the ultimate reference book. It's like reading product blogs versus reading *Consumer Reports*. Product blogs are based on the bloggers' experiences. They can be biased and one-sided, but they can also give you insight into a product. But *Consumer Reports* provides shoppers with product ratings and research. It is unbiased and unconstrained, and it truly helps shoppers make informed decisions. It is an advocate that calls for reliability and remedies, holding manufacturers responsible for their products and ensuring that those products meet or exceed industry standards. Sound familiar? The Bible is a reliable source that provides responses to any questions you have or solutions for any challenges you face. It holds us all accountable, and it advocates for us to uphold *its* standards. It is unbiased because it was written with all of us in mind, regardless of our pasts, problems, sins, and shortcomings. Its research dates back to the first woman, Eve, who started all the issues we face today as women (e.g., painful childbirth, sin, death, a first-class ticket out of Eden, and the occasional heartache that love can bring). I digress! So remember—*The Single Gal's Guide to Shopping for a Great Guy* is just my two cents' worth of advice. For more in-depth instruction, pick up the Bible!

Chapter 13

Sisters' Shopping List

Sisters,

Like any shopper who is preparing a list of what she needs to buy at a store, we too should keep a shopping list handy. But unlike our lengthy what-I-want-in-a-man lists, this list should be comprised of dreams, hopes, struggles,

115

hurts, triumphs, strategies, plans, and goals that we pray for, pursue, or want to push from our lives.

So let's create a shopping list together by doing the following:

- Share *The Single Gal's Guide* with your sisters and read it together.
- Scan back over your notes at the end of each chapter.
- Specify or summarize below those things you desire, the dreams you have, and the areas of your life, your dating relationships, and your friendships that you want to improve. This serves as your Sisters' Shopping List—a list of things that you should share with your sisters.

_____

_____

_____

_____

_____

- Spend time in prayer over your Sisters' Shopping List.
- Support your sisters by holding them accountable and by praying over the lists they have shared with you.

- Study God's Word regularly.
- Search for Bible verses that are applicable to your list.
- Send some of your prayer requests to me at thesinglegalsguide@gmail.com so that I can lift up your list to God in prayer!

Sincerely,

Your sis,

Tiff

Afterword: Shopping Tips

Attention, shoppers, ladies, gals, divas, lovelies, girls, beloveds, beauties, girlies, sistas, and friends.
We had a blast and some good laughs, but this shopping trip is nearing its end.
My prayer is that you were completely satisfied
after reading *The Single Gal's Guide*.
But before I wrap up this shopping trip,
I'd like to leave you with a few fun shopping tips.

1. We are still, in part, like the little girls who loved to play pretend. We still want the house, the car, the children, and the men. But instead of chasing the childhood dream, seek ye first the kingdom of God, and let Him provide everything you need. He has the power to exceed your dreams.

2. The Lord knows your every desire, your every want, like, and wish. Since He knows what's best for you and has planned your future, try trusting Him to write your single's shopping list.

3. Keep your "purse" buckled, locked, buttoned, or zipped. Only your husband deserves the valuables between those hips.

4. You were fearfully and wonderfully designed. So love yourself enough to remove the for-sale sign.

5. Stop digging through the clearance bin thinking that cheap and damaged is good enough. Instead, be a smart shopper who is wise, patient, and is willing to save up.

6. Good shopping pals are essential during any shopping trip. They'll tell you when your "merchandise" is too loose or too clingy on your hips. They love you enough to be honest, even when it offends. So surround yourself with good girlfriends.

7. Life's hurts, disappointments, and poor decisions can create baggage that we keep carrying with us throughout our lives. Let God carry those heavy, overstuffed bags, and watch Him make your burdens light.

8. Don't jump in the self-checkout lane just to hurry and get out the store. Let the Cashier check you

out. He knows how to help you find exactly what you need and are looking for.

9. Your purse is worth the wait! Ninety days is not an adequate expiration date. If he truly loves you, he won't need the refund policy. He will instead pay toward your value and add a lifetime warranty.

10. Spend a little time chatting online and getting to know a cyberdater, because he could be a creep, crook, someone else's husband, or a serial raper! Be open and honest and demand some respect. If you sense that he is computer fraud, block him and disconnect.

11. Realize that you too are expensive merchandise, especially in God's eyes. God valued and loved you enough to allow His Son to lay down His life. You are worth more than diamonds. You are deserving. You are precious. So don't sell yourself cheap. Make a man love and respect you, and take you from a single shopper to his wife!

Final Checkout: Closing the Deal

Question: So what happens when the single gal finds a great guy?

Answer: Girl, you run to the checkout and close the great deal, just like you would if you found a to-die-for dress or some must-be-heaven-sent high heels!

But seriously, here are seven things that I believe we should all do when we are confident we have found Mr. Right:

1. *As when buying a great pair of shoes, make sure you are a good match and a good fit for each other.*

   Who would ever go shopping for shoes and leave the store with a mismatched pair that hurt, just to say that she bought the shoes? We usually make sure the shoes are a great fit first. So if you think you've met your match, get to know him: his beliefs, his likes, his dislikes, his goals, his background, his friends, his family, etc. Talk to him and spend time with him to make sure he is a good match for you. Make sure you are totally comfortable with him, and that you can trust him. You may find that he is a great guy—but for someone else. That's okay too. It's important to take the time to discover if you are truly compatible. I think that women (especially those who are my age or older) are so ready for love that we try to make anything match, even when it is an obvious mismatch. Don't try to squeeze into a shoe that is a bad fit for you.

2. *Just like an expensive purse, maintain your quality.*

   We invest in expensive purses because we assume they are top quality, made of the best materials, and are built to last. Be that kind of woman – one who knows what she's made of, God's absolute best! Be a woman that he will be eager to invest in for the long run because he sees how much value she adds to him. Be a woman that he can build a lasting love and partnership with.

3. *Value him like you value your favorite piece of jewelry.*

   Ladies, you know how we treat that favorite necklace because we value it. We take extra special care of it. We treat it gently. Treat him like you treat that necklace. Show him that you value him by taking good care of him. It's okay to cook a meal, give a compliment, or buy a little gift or card to show that you care. Ask his opinion and let him know that you value his advice. Protect the secret things that he shares with you. Don't run around spreading his business, even to your shopping pals! Treat him with respect. Tell him what makes him so special to you.

4. *Know your role!*

Does the salesperson who specializes in shoes work in cosmetics? Of course not. He or she has his or her designated role. Ladies, know your role and stay in it. (I had to learn this for myself!) Let *him* be the man. Far too often, we independent women can act as if we don't need to be dependent on a man. Let's be real, ladies! There are lots of things that only a man can do for a woman (especially after you marry him!). In the meantime, let him open the door for you. Let him pay the bill. Let him make the first call. Let him make the first move (kisses only). Let him wash your car or mow your lawn. And, *ladies,* please let him propose! (Sorry, but I had to go there. I have seen so many stories on social media where the woman is down on one knee in front of the man. Call me old-fashioned or old-school or whatever you want, but too many of us are assuming the man's role and then getting mad when we feel he's not being the man in the marriage!)

5. *Date God's way, pray, and listen to what God has to say.*

When you need advice on a product, you typically find a salesperson or manager who knows the product and can either help you find it or make a recommendation, right? Who better to give a recommendation on Mr. Right than the one who created him and knows all about him? Consult the Almighty Matchmaker. Pray specifically that He will reveal what's not right about the man you believe is Mr. Right, or that He will confirm that Mr. Right is, in fact, "the one". Date God's way by waiting until marriage, even if you have had sex in the past. Commit to celibacy if you believe you've met "the one". (Premarital sex can become like rose-colored glasses that disguise things that you might need to see before you consider marriage. So wait until after the wedding. It will be worth it. *You* are worth the wait!) If you date God's way, pray and listen to what God has to say, He will let you know if you have really found your BAE. (That's for all of you who use that new term of endearment.)

6. *Date during normal shopping hours.*
   My advice and my personal rule is to date between normal shopping hours—ten in the morning to nine o'clock at night. The doors of stores are not open all night, and neither should you be. You can still be on the date after nine, but proceed with caution. Dates that don't begin until well after nine usually don't end until the next morning. So don't put yourself in a tempting situation. You are not a one-day doorbusting sale, honey!

7. ***Introduce him to your shopping pals.***

I know I told you not to involve too many people in your relationship, but do take him around to your good friends who you trust and who love you enough to give you good, honest advice. They might see or know something that you don't, *or* they might confirm that he is just as great a guy as you think he is! Remember—they know you and have your best interests at heart, even in the shopping cart.

About Tiff

My name is Tiffany Yvonne Grant, but as my good girlfriends do, you can refer to me as Tiff.

When I was thirty, God gave me the idea of writing a book for women like me—saved, single, and ready, waiting, begging, and praying to mingle. Seven years later, my dream has finally become a reality.

I am single and praying for a great Godly guy (complete with a ring - bling, plastic, or string).

I absolutely love the Lord, and I believe that He put me on this earth to share with, love on, inspire, encourage, empower, and entertain others through my personal testimony, writings, and music.

I am a native of San Antonio, Texas, where I proudly work in public education. I am a graduate of Texas A&M University, College Station, where I earned my bachelor of science in journalism; and Wayland Baptist University, San Antonio, where I earned my master's degree in business administration.

I am a singer, songwriter, and poet, and I released my solo gospel project, *Transformed,* in 2007.

I have two amazing parents, Stan and Enola, who have been married for over forty years. I believe in the institution of marriage, and I want that same kind of longstanding love. But while I wait, I want to show girls, young ladies, and women that we don't have to compromise ourselves and our beliefs to find love; that God forgives and redeems our mistakes; and that we are worth the time, energy, pursuit, and the wait! I also want all of you to know you don't have to meet the ideals of sex, beauty, and relationships that society tries to dictate. My hope and prayer is that this book accomplishes that goal in a faith-filled, fun, and fabulous way.

Enjoy, lovely ladies. Love y'all. And thank you so much for your support!

Tiff

Fine Print: If I am still single in a few more years, I might pull my list from the trash, iron it out, and update it. It might then look something like this!

The At-Least or No-More-Than List

- ✓ at least breathing on his own
- ✓ at least four of his original teeth
- ✓ at least has a job or receives a check for something (including from the state for being cray-cray-crazy!)
- ✓ no more than ten baby mamas and ten kids
- ✓ saved—a given!
- ✓ LOL. Just joking.

CPSIA information can be obtained
at www.ICGtesting.com
Printed in the USA
LVOW04s1259220416

484879LV00023B/287/P